DON'T BE AFRAID

C. A. HARMS

To all those who have loved and lost, the life you've built will live on in your heart forever. As well as the hearts of those you've touched.

PROLOGUE

S *awyer*

THE FIRST TIME I SAW PATRICK, ALL IT TOOK WAS one smile and I knew he would be my everything.

I was nineteen and he was older by five years and could have had his pick of anyone, but he chose me. But it wasn't the "sweep you off your feet," "happily ever after" kind of love. We had rough times, but we always came out the other end stronger.

Now here we sat, side by side, his hand in mine as I stared ahead at the scan of his abdomen pinned to a lit board. The mass in the center was so prominent that there was no way to miss it. I tried to keep it together, but I was terrified. My chest ached and my throat constricted more and more with each breath. My hands shook uncontrollably, but I ignored the fear. I had to.

"Head up, beautiful." I looked over at Patrick. Those

exhausted dark circles under his eyes only made the blue irises seem even bluer. I wanted to touch his handsome face, but I was frozen with fear. "We'll get through this," he assured me, but I could see the doubt in his eyes.

Unable to speak, I offered a nod, a forced smile, and a gentle squeeze of his hand.

The sound of the door to the small office opening had me jerk in surprise as my heart raced even faster. I'd lost track of how long we'd sat there with only our thoughts and our worries to keep us company.

Patrick and I watched as Dr. Sheppard walked around the side of his desk and took a seat in the leather chair behind it. The silence was deafening and did nothing to ease my mind.

The doctor's chest rose and fell a few times before he spoke, as if he, too, felt the anxiety and devastation of what he was about to share. "I'm so sorry, I wish I had better news." He looked across his desk at us with a solemn expression. "It's spread, Patrick, and not just to your liver."

"Okay, so…." Patrick's words lay heavy in the air as we waited for the doctor to proceed. When Patrick hung his head and took a deep calming breath, I knew what I'd hoped was a road ahead was actually a dead end. The racing fear and the deep ache inside me grew so strong that I knew I couldn't control them. I was falling apart.

"Isn't there a treatment of some kind?" Patrick sounded like he was struggling to keep a lid on his panic. "Something I can do? Anything?" He slid forward, staring at the doctor with hope, though he shook with what I'm sure was the same anxiety I felt.

The defeated look in Dr. Sheppard's eyes said it all. "Pancreatic cancer is typically diagnosed in the advanced stages. At that point, treatment isn't available. Those symptoms you've been experiencing, the weight loss, abdominal pain, even the slight yellowing of your skin, are all advance signs.

If you look at this"—he turned in his chair and pointed to the scan behind him—"your tumor is already a significant size. I truly wish there was something more we could do."

None of us spoke for a long time. Millions of things ran through my mind, paralyzing me with sadness and fear. Imagining a life without Patrick in it was like imagining a life without daylight. Agony like I had never felt before shot through me and breathing evenly was suddenly impossible.

"You have to fight." I spun in my seat to face my husband, gripping the arm of the chair so tight, my fingers ached. The fear in his eyes gutted me. Patrick had always been the strong one. He'd been the one to hold me up when I needed it. I couldn't process having our roles reversed. It all seemed so surreal.

"Patrick," I said in a tone that demanded his attention. When he finally looked directly at me, his eyes were glossy. I feel as if someone had set fire to my chest and the flames were consuming me. "You have to fight," I repeated in a hoarse whisper.

"Fight what, Sawyer?" He moved his hands out before him, fisting them and then releasing before gripping the arms of his own chair. "Please tell me, because maybe you heard something I didn't." His throat bobbed and his eyes closed tightly for a brief second and his lips pressed firmly together as he tried to fight his emotions. "What I heard was that I have no chance. What's to fight? Tell me, damn it, what's to fight?"

"I'm pregnant," I cried, tears rolling along my cheeks uncontrollably.

My heart shattered as his anger faded and he went limp. He leaned back, his shoulders sagged in defeat.

I slid from my chair and knelt before him. Placing one hand on both of his knees, I could barely speak clearly, but I gave it my best. "You have to fight, Patrick. You have to." I

4 | C. A. HARMS

couldn't accept him not being here. I wouldn't. The idea that there was nothing left to do wasn't acceptable. "Fight for me and for our baby. You have to. We need you." I laid my head in his lap, repeating those words over and over as I broke. "We need you."

We were supposed to do this together. Raise a family, love one another until we were old and gray. That had always been our plan.

Any amount of control I had left vanished the second his fingers combed through my hair and he whispered, "I'm sorry," just before his own sobs filled the room.

CHAPTER 1

We drove in silence, our hands joined on the center console. Talking seemed pointless now, but I think we both desperately needed the connection.

The man I love, my best friend and the father of my unborn child, had only a short time left to live. I felt as if this were all my fault. Should I have seen that something was wrong? Noticed a change in him that would trigger concern? It was my job to take care of him and I failed.

The cancer had metastasized, meaning it had passed through his bloodstream and spread to his liver and stomach. This left little hope that Patrick would live to see the birth of our child. Each time I allowed myself to think that far ahead, panic rose inside me all over again.

The doctor suggested that we try chemotherapy to reduce pain, which may allow him to also maintain nutrition, but the side effects would be brutal. Patrick had also declined the option to receive an abdominal port for drug treatment. It was difficult to hear my husband insist on living out the remainder of his life as God intended, not weakened or destroyed by the side effects chemo or other drug treatments would inflict. As we left the doctor's office, my mind kept screaming, *Why?*, and I couldn't help but be angry that he wouldn't even try.

I wanted to be selfish. I wanted to be told that there was something that would give him more time. I wanted to hear that this was all just a huge mistake and he'd still be here when our child had their first birthday, or even on their first day of school. I knew I was being ridiculous, but I just couldn't accept that I'd soon be living without the man who in my eyes hung the moon. Patrick made everything brighter. He gave me hope at times when I thought all hope was lost. He was my rock, and without him at my side, the foundation for my life was crumbling beneath me.

"I think we should take a trip."

He slowed the car as we approached the gravel drive that led to our home, and I looked over at him as he slowly made the turn onto it. I expected to see sadness in his eyes but was met with a smile instead.

"Anywhere you wanna go. Hawaii, Jamaica, you name it."

When he placed the vehicle in Park, I turned in the seat to face him. "You need to rest," I stated, feeling as if it was something he should already know. "You need to take it easy, and taking a trip isn't getting rest."

"I don't want to rest."

"That's the problem, you never do," I snapped. It was wrong but I couldn't control my anger. "You always overdo it. You overworked yourself into an early grave. Why didn't you pay closer attention to the signs, Patrick, why?" He remained silent as if he knew I needed this outburst. "Maybe if you'd paid attention, they could have caught it sooner. But instead you kept working and ignored everything."

When he still said nothing, I reached for the handle and opened the door, practically falling out of his truck. The stupid thing was so big, I'd misjudged the distance to the ground. Damn thing was completely ridiculous.

The sound of his door slamming shut only enhanced my need to flee. I needed space. I needed to run off somewhere where I could pretend this wasn't happening.

"Sawyer, wait," Patrick hollered and instantly I stopped, my knees weakening as exhaustion finally hit me. I turned and stared back at him, my world shattering around me, and no matter how hard I cried, not matter how angry I got, it wouldn't change what our future held.

"Why?" I cried, unable to stop myself. "Nothing about any of this is fair."

Patrick closed the distance between us and brushed his fingers along my cheek. As if I hadn't already felt defeated, that simple touch shook me to my core. Those touches were now limited, just as everything else was between us. Our kisses, our laughter, the way he held me close at night as if he was protecting me from all the evil in the world, it was all now a simple countdown to the end.

I would live every moment from now until then wondering if it would be his last. How could I not? I'd never felt so empty. Patrick always made sure I knew how special I was to him each day. Now here I was, trying to imagine what life would be like without all the things from him that I treasured most.

"I won't get through this," I whispered as I closed my eyes, unable to look at the pain in his gaze. I was weak, I'll admit it. "I can't do this without you. I can't wake up every day knowing you're not by my side."

"You can." I shook my head and rested my cheek over his heart. The gentle rap of the steady beat somehow gave me a small sliver of peace. "Our child will need you."

My heart broke all over again at his words. "I'm not

strong enough," I whispered, fisting his shirt, unable to let him go.

"You're wrong." I closed my eyes with every intention of arguing with him, but he continued before I could speak. "You always say it's my strength that bonds us, and I've never argued with you. But now I'm going to, because, Sawyer, it's you, baby. It's always been you. Your light, your kindness, and your determination are what never let us fail. I know those things are gonna hold you together through this too. I know it'll be hard, but you'll make it."

I couldn't speak. My throat was so raw and my chest ached with such an immense amount of emotion that I couldn't remember ever feeling so depleted.

"I need you to promise me something."

"Don't," I said through gritted teeth. "Don't you dare make me promise things to you like you'll be gone tomorrow."

"But this is something I need from you now." When I only curled into him, accepting the comfort he offered when he wrapped me in his arms, he continued. "I need you to promise me that we'll live the time we have left together without reservations. Promise me that we'll live it fully, no complaining, no lecturing. Just give me this time to love you and love every moment with you without pause."

My tears fell so heavy, his shirt became damp beneath my cheeks.

"I don't want to live the days I have left as if they are my last. Instead, I want to create so many memories that it'll be impossible for you to forget me."

"Don't say that," I demanded, finally lifting my head to look up at him. "I'll never forget you."

He pressed a gentle kiss to my lips before resting his forehead to mine. "Promise me."

A moment of silence passed, and I wanted to say yes more

than anything, but the hurt and sadness lying heavy on my heart made it impossible to speak.

"Today we'll fall apart," Patrick assured me. "Today we'll blame God, we'll hate our fate, we'll yell, cuss, and scream. We'll be angry and sad. Today we'll do all that." I nodded because I could do that. In fact, I already was. "But tomorrow, we live."

The idea of living felt almost impossible to face right now, though. Living meant we were one day closer to the day he'd no longer be here. I didn't want to live, damn it. I wanted to freeze time and keep him, right here, right now, forever.

"Tomorrow we live," I whispered, even though the words felt like acid. I knew he needed them, but they broke me even more.

CHAPTER 2

I was spent, yet I still couldn't give in to my body's desire to sleep. Closing my eyes meant missing time with him, and I couldn't do that. Even though he was curled toward me in bed, a soft snore falling from his lips, I still couldn't let go.

Today we'd cried more tears than I think either of us ever had, and shared the news with those we love. I sat there while Perry and Luann, Patrick's parents, sobbed and held their son, wishing for a different outcome. I accepted their hugs and gave them in return, though their attempts at comfort still left me feeling empty. The news of our baby was something I had chosen to hold back for now, but Patrick used the joy of our pregnancy as a way to bring happiness to a sad situation.

I wanted to be joyful, truly I did, and I'm sure one day I will be, but today I just couldn't. Today the only thing my pregnancy reminded me of was that Patrick wouldn't be here to raise our child with me.

Through the darkness I could see the gentle curve of his nose and the strong line of his jaw, and I wanted so badly to touch him, but I refrained. I didn't want my touch to wake him. I knew had he been awake, he would only attempt to lure me to sleep, and I couldn't. Too many things were running around in my mind. So instead, I kept perfectly still, counted his breaths, and smiled when each snore was followed by that weird little gurgling noise I used to get so annoyed by. It was strange how the things that once drove me insane about him were the things I treasured now.

He always used to say that one day I'd miss his snoring, and I would, of course, tell him I wouldn't. God, how wrong I was. I would miss everything about him, the good, the bad, and the annoying.

I'd promised to live tomorrow, and I dreaded keeping that promise. It would be one of the hardest things I'd ever had to do. I felt like we were living on borrowed time, like I was watching the sand fall through the hourglass and another piece of my soul was fading away with each grain.

My mind slowly drifted back to the day we met, when this man managed to knock me on my ass with a simple smile and a hello. Thinking of it still gave me goose bumps.

I WALKED ACROSS THE PARKING LOT TOWARD THE DINER AND stumbled when I saw a man climbing out of a big blue truck. He had long legs, and a narrow waist that V'd up toward a fit chest that strained against his red T-shirt.

When he looked in my direction, heat rose to my cheeks as I realized he'd noticed me staring. I fully expected him to dismiss me as just another goggle-eyed girl, but instead he offered a smile that only made me blush harder. He was gorgeous, and I was floored that he was staring back at me.

"Hello." He fisted his keys in his hand and took a step toward me.

"Hi." That simple word took so much effort. I felt like I had been tackled and all the air had been knocked out of me.

"We could both stand here all morning and stare at one another"—his grin widened as he tilted his head slightly and looked me over from head to toe—"but from the looks of it, you're on your way to work, and I'd hate for you to get in trouble because of me."

I shook my head, attempting to clear the fog that had filled it. "Yeah," I said with a nervous laugh that only made me feel more embarrassed, "I should get inside."

I hurried to the door and tried to ignore the way he watched me.

"I'm Patrick, by the way." I looked back over my shoulder at the sound of his voice, and damn that smile of his made me weak in the knees. "Just in case you're wondering."

"Sawyer."

He arched his brow in interest, and I knew he was curious about my name. Everyone always was. I grew up in foster care, knowing nothing of my biological family or why they had given me that name. All anyone had ever told me was that I'd been placed in the care of the state at the moment of my birth. From there I was passed around from one place to the next for years until I was placed with an older couple who cared for me until I was old enough to be on my own. After Harvey Miller, my foster dad, passed, the only family I had left was Rachel, my mother.

"I like it," he said with that same mesmerizing smile, and I looked away wondering how one smile from a man I didn't know could hit me so deep.

THAT SMILE STILL DID THE SAME THING TO ME. IT made me weak in moments of anger and managed to flip a terrible situation into a better one. I closed my eyes. The fear of one day not being able to remember that smile hit me so hard, a sob broke free before I could control it. Panic rushed in, and I got out of bed and went to the door that led to the hallway. Covering my mouth, I continued toward the kitchen and braced my hands against the edge of the countertop.

I held back my sobs as best I could, though my chest shook with each attempt. Hanging my head, I closed my eyes, then jumped in surprise when Patrick's chest pressed firmly against my back. He engulfed me in his arms and held me while I cried.

"Let it go, baby," he whispered near my ear. I was shocked that I still had tears left to shed, but I did. My heart was shattered, and my faith was gone. All those little comforts that make life bearable meant nothing to me now. I would live each day in darkness with only the clothes on my back, without even the smallest complaint if I could still have Patrick by my side. All I needed was him. All I wanted was him.

"This is gonna break me," I whispered through my sobs as I turned in his arms to face him. "I don't know how I'm gonna get through this."

"You will," he assured me. When I shook my head, he gripped my cheeks and held my face firmly. "You'll be strong when you need to be, but for now you can fall apart."

I knew that was hard for him to say because his lips trembled as he looked into my eyes, trying to stay strong for me.

"I'm scared," I confessed. "I don't know how to be me without you." It was a weak confession, but it was true, and when I said it, he fell apart too. His chest shook as his owns sobs broke free and he squeezed me just a little tighter, seeking the same comfort I, too, was needy for.

Patrick had met me when I was just a girl who'd been forced to grow up long before I should have had to. He understood how alone I felt and how much loss I'd gone through, and he stood beside me in my bad times and accepted all my faults. He was the foundation I'd built my life on over the last five years, and without him, I didn't know how to live.

CHAPTER 3

A week passed filled with many tears along with the laughter I'd promised him. Though I couldn't help but feel I shouldn't be laughing when I was watching my husband slowly fade before me.

I could see the change in him daily. The strong, proud man I'd fallen in love with now looked frail and exhausted. I knew he was forcing himself to stay alert, fearful of missing too much, when the exhaustion threatened to overtake him, and that frustrated me. He needed rest, but he refused to let his illness consume him.

I sat on the porch swing, looking out over our backyard with a warm blanket wrapped around me and a cup of hot tea in my hands. I'd long ago given up on my attempt at reading, and instead watched Patrick and his best friend Gage sitting on the tailgate of his truck in the driveway.

Gage had been here almost every day to help with house-work or yardwork. We'd bought this old farmhouse thinking we'd fill our home and yard with our children and grandchildren one day. It wasn't huge, but three acres was a lot of space for just one woman to tend to. A four-bedroom home was a lot too, but I loved this place and the historical feeling it had. The original woodwork, the old squeaky floor, and the wobbly banister all gave it character. But now I wondered if I shouldn't just suggest we sell it.

Those feelings always led to me hating myself for acting as if he was already gone.

"You doing okay?"

I looked to my left to find Gage standing only a few feet away and realized just how lost in my own thoughts I'd been. I hadn't noticed him moving toward the porch or heard him walk up the old stairs that were only a few feet away.

"I'm good," I lied, and from the way he looked at me with his forehead wrinkled, I knew he was aware of it too. "Okay, I'm as good as I'm gonna get."

Gage looked across the yard to where Patrick was picking away at the old paint on the fence. He'd decided he was going to do all he could to fix this place up to ensure I wouldn't have to. I wished he wouldn't, but it was something he felt he had to do, so I didn't argue.

"I know the two of you are trying to be strong and hold it together for each other and I admire that. But I'm gonna tell you the same thing I told him." Gage turned back to me, trying to fight off the tears glimmering in his eyes. "I don't give a shit what time of day or night it is, I'm here for both of you. This is a lot to take on, and I'm having a hard time with it too. But, Sawyer, just know either of you can ask me for anything."

Gage and Patrick were like brothers. They had been insep`arable since birth, and I knew losing Pat was going to devastate him.

"Thank you." I nodded as I took a calming breath. "I promise not to occupy too much of your time, though. I wouldn't want Honor getting upset and missing you."

I was trying to lighten the mood and maybe make him

smile, but it backfired. "She'll be all right as long as she's got her nail appointment every Tuesday and her coffee with the girls every morning." The girls were the group of stuck-up snobs who met daily to gossip at the local café. Honor was born and bred in Tuscaloosa. She was the former Miss Alabama and she carried herself as such. She and I were cordial, but I knew she thought I was beneath her. I didn't let it get to me, though, because I knew that a girl like her needed attention; girls like me did not. The only attention I desired was Patrick's. I didn't need to turn heads as I walked down the street.

Though I always wondered why Gage's attention wasn't good enough for her. He was a good-looking man who carried himself with that same confidence and strength Patrick always had. It was a shame Honor couldn't see what a prize she had.

"Well, in that case, you can hang out here all you want."

He winked as he moved toward the back door. "Gotta get your boy and myself a cold one."

When the back door closed, I looked back toward Patrick, who waved for me to come over. I stood, placed my blanket on the swing, and tucked my hands into the sleeves of my sweatshirt as I walked to him.

As I got closer, he pulled off his gloves and slid them into his back pocket. "You mean you don't have this done yet," I teased and gained that smile of his I loved so much.

"Well that would be your fault." I arched my brow and he hooked my waist. "You keep distracting me from my work. A pretty lady all cozied up under a blanket puts ideas in a man's head."

"Oh really?"

"Really."

I moved in for a kiss and he bit my lower lip and gave it a little teasing tug instead. "I can't get a thing done because the only thing I keep thinking about is me and you under that blanket rolling around in front of the fire."

"That sounds promising." I leaned in and went for the kiss he denied me only moments ago. "Dinner in front of the fire," I offered and he wagged his eyebrows. "I meant real food."

"Now you're just teasing." His little pout made me laugh.

"Who says I'm teasing?" I leaned in close to his ear. "I thought I could be dessert."

The little growl that escaped him pleased me. We hadn't had many moments like this since that day in the doctor's office, and it was mainly my fault. I'd spent almost every waking moment feeling as if the weight of a thousand men was pressed against my chest. But we both desperately needed times like this to remind us of who we were before that horrid day'.

As I stepped away and turned back toward the house, he slapped my ass. "Give me a couple hours and you better be ready."

I didn't say anything more, because Gage had rejoined us. Instead, I moved back toward the house, feeling almost excited about what lay ahead for our evening.

THE FIRE WAS LIT, AND A SMALL TRAY OF FRUIT, cheeses, and crackers sat out on the table in the center of our living room rug. On the side closest to the fireplace, I'd placed our large throw pillows upon a big blanket.

When Patrick entered the living room, freshly showered and wearing only a pair of pajama pants, I stopped what I was doing just to simply look at him. Though he'd lost some weight, he was still the most perfect man I had ever seen. He smiled, and the place inside me that only he could touch ached immensely.

"You have no idea how beautiful you are." It was like he'd taken the words from my mouth, only I'd been thinking them about him.

As he walked farther into the room, he took in the table, the food, and my glass of water sitting next to his ice-cold bottle of beer. No matter how hard I'd tried, I could never get him to enjoy a glass of Moscato as much as I did. He was a beer man through and through. I laughed to myself just thinking about all my failed attempts at pushing a glass of wine at him over the years.

"What's so funny?"

I looked up just as he reached me and slowly joined me on the floor.

"I was remembering that face you make every time I try to get you to drink just one glass of wine with me." He faked a shiver and his lip curled as if he, too, remembered it. "Yeah," I laughed, pointing at his mouth, "that one."

"I'd do just about anything for you and you know that," he reminded me. "But that is one thing I can never learn to love."

We sat before the fire, talking and laughing. It was almost as if the last week hadn't happened. I think he felt it too as he looked back at me, an expression of peace almost covering his face.

He reached out, took the glass from my hand, and placed it on the table beside us. He prowled closer, using the weight of his body to nudge me back. Together we lowered ourselves to the floor, our eyes locked on one another's.

"I've always loved this exact moment." He skimmed the side of his nose along the side of mine. "The way you look at me right before I kiss you. That longing in your eyes, that need. Or the way your lips take on that pouty look, parting just slightly, I love that too. It drives me out of my mind."

I closed my eyes when he kissed me softly.

Patrick had always been a passionate guy who freely spoke whatever was on his mind. It was one of the things I loved most about him. His words made me feel beautiful and mesmerizing.

I opened my eyes once more as he kissed along the side of my neck, then moved lower, above the swell my breast as he carefully gathered the material of my shirt. He paused over my stomach and slowly placed his hand over it.

My chest tightened and my throat swelled, and it was all I could do to hold back the tears. This was a moment of acceptance for both of us. Our baby hadn't been a topic of discussion, and part of me felt guilty for it. But the excitement was there, only it was hidden by the sadness.

He slid his palm along my stomach before curling it around my side, then leaning closer and pressing a kiss just below my belly button. No longer able to fight the emotions building inside me, I let a tear fall.

When he looked up at me and I saw the matching shine in his eyes, I knew he felt that same ache. The unfairness of it all and the fact he'd miss so much angered me. He had an amazing life he'd built and everything to live for, but that choice had been taken from him and there was nothing we could do about it.

I just wanted the life I'd dreamed of, and I wanted him here to share it all.

CHAPTER 4

P *atrick*

LEANING BACK AGAINST THE FENCE, I TOOK A moment just to breathe. It was growing a little harder each day to get through the day doing the same things I used to. Just a little activity made me feel tired and weak, and it was difficult to face. It was hard to accept that one day soon, I'd be unable to take care of Sawyer the way I'd promised I always would.

"Hey, man." I lifted my head, fighting the urge to break down, and saw Gage look up at me from his work. I hesitated before saying, "Can I ask you something?"

He lowered the sander and brushed the dust from his hands as he stood. "Anything."

Gage was amazing. He was a man of his word, a solid, genuine guy I was proud to call my best friend.

"I know this a lot to ask, because you have Honor and a life of your own—"

"I don't care what it is, Pat. You know I got you. Whatever you need."

I took a deep breath, trying to calm the swarm of despair taking me over. "Can you watch out for her?" Asking this of my best friend broke my heart, but I needed to do it. I had to know she'd be okay. Not knowing what would happen to her was the hardest part of all this. "I know she'll say she's fine, that she doesn't need help, but she will. She pretends to accept this, but at night I still hear her cry. Fuck, Gage, her eyes are swollen every morning and it nearly guts me. I can barely breathe knowing she's gonna fall apart and I won't be here to hold her together."

"The moment you married Sawyer, she became my family too." I could see that assurance I needed in his eyes. "This is gonna tear us all apart, Pat. Hell, I don't remember a part of my life you weren't there for, so I think I'll need her to hold me up just the same as she'll need me."

"Don't let her push everyone away, because she'll try. It's who she is." Gage knew this already. He'd seen us through a couple rough times and had witnessed her attempts to close herself off when something bad happened. "There's just no one else I trust more, ya know. It's not only gonna be her I'm leaving behind." Those words burned my throat. My beautiful wife was going to have to face losing me while being thrust into single-parenting life.

"I know it's nowhere near the same, but I promise you I'll watch over the both of them."

A moment of silent acceptance passed between us. No words were necessary. We'd always been there for one another, and though this was the hardest of times, Gage's word was his bond. He'd watch over Sawyer and he'd watch over our child as if they were his own.

I STOOD UNDER THE FALL OF WARM WATER FROM the showerhead. The pelting drops massaged my scalp and I closed my eyes. Everything I wanted to do and all the things I wanted to ensure were done just kept piling up.

I'd put everything off over the years, just as most of us do, and I wanted to take care of Sawyer and the things around our home that needed to be finished while I still could. But now I only had a limited amount of time left. I didn't know how I'd feel this time next week, let alone next month. I'd looked at the statistics when Sawyer wasn't around, and the chances of me being here this time next year were slim.

Putting on a brave face was torturous at times. I wanted to break—fuck, I wanted to hit something and go crazy with rage over being handed this death sentence, but I knew it would accomplish nothing. So instead, I woke up every day, held my wife, kissed her softly, and made yet another day count.

Inside, it was a constant battle, though. It was a nightmare knowing that one day she'd wake up and the place where I once lay beside her would be empty. Knowing that her tears would fall heavy and I won't be here to kiss them away.

I could choose to go through chemotherapy, but if I did, I knew I would spend the time I had left feeling even more like shit than I already did. So I chose to live out the days I had left without drugs making me sick and weak.

Honestly, though, was either choice better? I was gonna die either way. I was gonna leave behind everyone and everything I love. Life would go on, they would all move forward, and I'd miss it all.

As I tilted my head back, I allowed the water to run over my face, hiding the tears that had begun to escape as anxiety took over. I wasn't even aware I was sobbing until Sawyer's voice echoed through the bathroom.

The shower curtain moved to the side to reveal my wife, looking worried. Without a second thought, I hooked my arm around her shoulders and pulled her toward me. Fully clothed, shoes and all, she came willingly and wrapped her arms around me tight.

"I'm gonna miss everything, Sawyer," I said with my face buried in her wet hair as it stuck to my lips. "I know we haven't talked about the baby. I understand why we've both avoided it, but—"

"Stop." She squeezed me tighter. "I can't."

"There's a chance I won't be here when it—"

"I said stop," she repeated, louder this time.

Pushing back, I forced her to look at me. "No, we need to face this. We both need to accept that it's a strong possibility."

"I don't want to face it," she declared with that stubborn look in her eyes that she always gets. They narrowed as her forehead wrinkled. "I can't."

We both stared at one another without speaking. The harder I pushed, the worse it was gonna get, but ignoring the inevitable wasn't gonna make it go away. "We have to."

"No, we don't," she shouted, and her words echoed through the bathroom. "Facing that means I have to give up the little hope I have left. The hope that by some miracle, you'll be here. I need that hope, Patrick." Sawyer's lower lip trembled and heaviness filled my chest. "I need it so bad and I can't give it away. I won't. In my mind, I see you here with me as we look at our child together, counting her little fingers or his tiny toes. I need that. It's holding me together, okay? If I give that hope up, if I let go of that image in my mind, I'll fall." She took a deep breath. "Let me keep that hope."

I couldn't deny her. So instead I nodded and pulled her to me once more, and together we stood beneath the fall of the warm water. I'm not sure how long we stayed there. I just knew that with her near, her body pressed firmly to my own, I felt whole.

CHAPTER 5

S *awyer*

"HOW ARE YOU DOING?" WILLOW, PATRICK'S SISTER, asked as I set my cup of hot chocolate on the table before taking a seat across from her. "And before you say you're fine, remember I know you well enough to know you're lying."

Willow was older than Patrick and was recently divorced with no children. She was more of a free spirit than the rest of her immediate family, which I believe was why her marriage didn't work out. She traveled the world and volunteered in other countries after disasters hit. She was also heavily into her church and faith, which I found inspiring. Though she might not have been around often, we talked a few times a week. She was the sister I never had.

"I'm not okay," I confessed, "but I'm holding it together the best I can. I know I can't change things, and I know it's important to cherish every moment, so that's what I'm doing."

"Okay, so in front of Pat you do that." She leaned in and placed her hand over mine, gently squeezing it. "But when you're with me, let go." I bit the inside of my cheek as I tried to hold back my emotions. "Get angry, cry, blame God and everyone else you want. If you need to throw things, then throw them. Just don't hold it in, Sawyer. Please feel, you have to, sweetheart, because if you try to be this strong, held-together version of yourself all the time, it's gonna hit you so hard, it's gonna cripple you."

"I already feel numb," I confessed. "Like I'm stuck in some recurring nightmare where I wake up, smile, and move through my day only to repeat it again the next day. But I don't wanna smile, I don't wanna laugh. I just want to curl up with Patrick in bed and cry. I wanna go back to when I first met him and change it all. I want to force him to go to the doctor sooner."

Willow said nothing, allowing me to say all the things rolling around in my mind, even though some of them may have sounded crazy.

"The other night I actually dreamed that this entire thing was a dream. It all seemed so real. After I woke up, I lay there staring up at the ceiling, analyzing everything that had happened, and for the first time I felt like the weight of it all just lifted. The sadness, the anger, it was all gone." I shook my head, laughing at how ridiculous it seemed now. "I looked over at Pat and actually smiled at him as I listened to him snore. I remember thinking I would never again complain about his snoring. I allowed myself to believe that the dream was meant to remind me of how lucky I was to have the life I have. Then my gaze landed on the medication sitting on his nightstand."

Willow nodded, urging me to go on.

"Then it all came rushing back: the doctor telling us, then him telling his parents. Gage crying in his hands when Patrick and I shared the news with him. That crushing feeling came back, like it was all happening all over again. I don't know how I'm gonna do this. He says I'm strong, Willow, but I'm not. I'm falling apart with each day, and I swear to you I'm not gonna make it through this. I don't see how I can."

"For him." I focused on the dedication in her stare, which was so much like her brother's. "We do it for him, and for his memory. We hold on to every part of him we can and make sure his child knows what a wonderful man he was. We remember each day that he loved us, and that is the greatest blessing. Through us, Patrick lives on."

She was right, but I still didn't accept the situation the way she had. I had so much rage inside me that at times I even scared myself. And having no one to be angry at only made it worse. I had no one I could lash out at, no one to punish, so the anger continued to smolder and I could feel it consuming me at times.

WHEN I LEFT THE GROCERY STORE, I TOOK THE longer way home, just needing a few more minutes to myself. At this point everyone around town who knew us, knew what we were facing. I hated the looks of pity I got from them.

Running into Honor was the worst part about today's trip. I couldn't help but wonder what Gage could possible see in such a cold woman.

"I'm sorry to hear about what y'all are facing." She'd reached out and placed her hand on my shoulder. "But could you do me a favor and pass along to my husband that it sure would be nice if he got a few things done around our own home for a change?"

Part of me wanted to slap her, and another part just felt sorry for her. She had a healthy husband and her whole life spread out before her, but she was so superficial that she couldn't pause for a moment and see just how lucky she was.

By the time I pulled into my driveway, dusk had fallen and the twinkling lights hanging from the trees caught my attention. They were strung from our porch on the east side of the house, intertwined throughout the two trees next to it, then draped over the awning of our shed.

Ignoring the bags still in the back, I climbed out of my car and moved toward the lights. As I rounded the shed, I found Gage and Patrick draping sheer white fabric over a small arch that wasn't there when I left a few hours ago.

"What's this?"

They both looked up from their task and smiled. "This is my best recreation of our wedding." The gleaming smile that took over Pat's face made me laugh. But this time it wasn't forced like usual, but a full-fledged, honest release of pure joy. "I know it's nowhere near as beautiful as the Swan House but—"

"It's amazing," I assured him, stunned at the effort they'd gone to.

We'd decided to get married in the evening at the gazebo overlooking the water near the garden of the most beautiful wedding venue I'd ever visited. The bridge that led us to that very spot had been lined with twinkling lights and they were strung throughout the gazebo, making the event even more intimate. Lanterns floated in the water and each person at our wedding held a flameless candle.

These two guys had taken the time to create the best replica they could with the space and materials they could find.

"I have groceries in the car," I said out of nowhere.

Gage stepped forward. "I got 'em."

"Wait." I spun around and watched him walk away. "You don't have to."

He paused and looked back over his shoulder. "You go spend some time with your guy. I got this." Looking past me, he nodded at Patrick. "Catch you tomorrow, and we can finish up that last coat of paint on the fence." He moved around the side of the house and was gone.

Our wedding song filled the emptiness and chills covered my arms and shoulders as I once again focused on my husband. "I can't believe you did all this."

"I wanted to remind you of the times before."

I knew what he meant, and I refused to let sadness take away from this moment. "So you gonna ask a girl to dance, or are you just gonna stand there staring at me?" I crossed my arms over my chest, trying to be sassy. When he offered me a grin with his brow arched, I knew I'd accomplished the look I was going for.

He held out his hand toward me, still grinning wide. "Can I have this dance, pretty lady?"

"I don't know," I said, uncrossing my arms and placing them on my hips instead. "Is that all I get, one?"

"You can have as many as you want, babe," he said, still holding his hand out to me as I moved in close. "We can dance all night if that's what you want."

I knew if I said that was exactly what I wanted, he'd do his best to give it to me. "I just want this, us," I whispered as I looked up at him, my chest pressed firmly to his. "For tonight, I want to pretend we have forever."

The words made it hard to hold back my tears, but I'd done it. Patrick nodded because I think he needed to pretend even more than I needed to. Then without any further delay we began to move to the music just as we had on our wedding night.

"You've still got the moves, Mr. Cooper." His chest shook

against mine as he chuckled. "And you still manage to make even the simplest dance feel like a tease." I didn't miss how his eyes took on a lustful haze. "And you tried to convince me that you didn't know how to dance."

"I didn't," he insisted. "I just went with my best friend's suggestions."

"Oh really? And what suggestions would those be?" Nothing about Gage and Patrick's interactions would surprise me. They had caused a great amount of trouble in their younger years, and instead of moving on from it, they only seemed to get worse as they got older. Like two kids trapped in grown men's bodies.

"He told me on the night before our wedding to imagine I was slowing making love to my girl when we danced. That it was just the two of us, her staring back at me with nothing but love and devotion in her eyes." I was surprised to hear that advice had come from Gage. I still found it hard to imagine him and Honor ever sharing any type of intimacy. In fact, I rarely saw them together. "He did, however, tell me I shouldn't think of you naked while doing so, because the guests didn't need to see the groom sporting wood."

I laughed because I could most definitely imagine Gage saying that.

"So that's why dancing with you has always felt more like long, torturous foreplay?" He nodded. "I'll admit, that may be the best piece of advice he's ever given you."

"No." Patrick leaned in and his lips skimmed over mine in a teasing manner that had me chasing after him for more. "The night I dropped you off after our third date, I went to his place." Pat kissed my jaw before leaning back to look into my eyes. "I told him that even though I'd only met you a few weeks ago, I just knew that you were the woman I was meant to fall in love with."

My eyes widened. He'd never shared this with me before

and I was at a loss. I was almost desperate to know more as I looked at him.

"He told me that if after only a few weeks you already had me feeling things that strong, then I'd better grab on tight and never let go." He lifted his left hand to cup my cheek as we swayed to the music in the background. "So I took his advice and got back in my truck and drove back to your place."

"You scared the hell out of me beating on my door like there was an alien invasion or something."

"That was the night everything changed," he whispered. "The moment you let me inside your apartment and looked up at me the way you did, I knew I would do just about anything to ensure you'd be mine forever."

We'd made love that night for the first time, throughout the evening and well into the morning. I remembered the way he held me, the way he looked at me as if he'd just been gifted the world.

"That was the best advice Gage ever offered me," Pat said before his lips pressed to mine and we got lost in one another.

As we stood beneath the lights that glimmered in the darkness, together we managed to forget all that lay ahead. We reconnected in a way that I think we both desperately needed, finding that part of us that had gotten buried beneath all that darkness. We found the love we'd built our lives on. We found that solid ground that made us feel whole.

CHAPTER 6

P atrick

KISSING HER HAD ALWAYS GIVEN ME THIS WEIRD sense of peace. Like I was home, safe and secure, and nothing could ever touch me. That hadn't changed; Sawyer was my solace.

Her skin was damp, and her chest felt as if it were fused to mine as I hovered above her, my weight supported by my forearms as pleasure took over her features. As I slowly moved my hips against hers, her lips parted just before she bit her lower lip and lifted her hips to meet mine.

Her body tightened around me as she chased her release and prolonged it at the same time. Like she wanted it so bad, but the taunting of its approach pleased her too.

Sawyer was gorgeous, though she never acted as though she was. I honestly think the fact she didn't realize it made her even more appealing. Her compassion and strength were what made me fall in love with her so quickly. Her beauty was just a bonus.

"I love you," I whispered, knowing the words would cause her to open her eyes and look at me. I loved seeing the look in them when she reached her peak. It was like an addiction. "You consume me; you always have."

I moved against her a little faster and her eyes began to close. "Look at me." I needed to see her. "Show me."

She knew what I meant.

She cupped the back of my neck with her hands, and her fingertips dug into my flesh. Her hips moved faster against mine, and her legs tightened around me seconds before she let go. A slow moan escaped her and I continue to move, feeling her pulsate around me. All the while her eyes remained locked on mine, and I could no longer hold back my own release.

My guttural moan echoed throughout the darkness of our bedroom and I fisted the sheet on either side of her head as my toes curled.

Over the last couple of weeks, we'd managed to find our groove once again, not only sexually but emotionally. Yes, we still had rough times, those moments when we'd both realized I would one day be absent from her life. Those moments were tough, but together we'd gotten through them.

This part, though, where we'd both get lost in one another, was one of my favorite times. We'd manage to forget, even if only for a little while, and just feel.

I took a few minutes to savor her body's reaction to lovemaking before I rolled to my side and ensured her body stayed tucked in close to mine with my palm resting against her stomach.

Five weeks ago I found out I was going to be a father. At that point, she was already close to six weeks along. It was hard to believe she was almost into to her second trimester.

I'd noticed her breasts becoming a little fuller, her belly a little rounder. It wasn't enough of a change to show if she was fully clothed, but when we were like this, I could see.

"What do you think we're gonna have?" I asked as I traced around her belly button with the tip of my finger. "Boy or girl?"

"A boy," she replied with certainty that surprised me. I would have thought she'd want a girl. "One who looks just like you."

"What if I want a little girl who looks just like you?"

"One day we could have—" She quickly averted her eyes. I'd done the same thing a time or two. I'd thought of something way off in the future and talked of how I couldn't wait for it. It was still hard to accept that my time was limited, and even harder because we couldn't know just how long I had left.

"You still could, you know." The idea made my stomach feel hollow, but I knew it was a possibility. She was young and beautiful and had a whole life ahead of her. Men noticed her. I'd seen it.

"Are you kidding me?" She looked at me with irritation, as if I'd just told her she should run out now and find a new man. "I can't believe you."

She tried to move away from me, but I held on to her, refusing to let her escape. "Wait, I'm just saying that someday, far away from now, you could fall in love again and have more children."

"Just stop." She turned her face away and I wished I'd kept my mouth shut.

"Okay, I'm sorry." I cupped her jaw and turned her to face me once more. "I have one more thing to say, then we won't talk about it anymore." She narrowed her eyes and I couldn't control the laughter that spilled from me. I immediately realized my mistake. Laughing at her when she's pissed is like throwing gasoline on a raging fire.

She scurried away and I slid across the bed and hurried after her. "I didn't mean to laugh," I said, still feeling the humor bubble inside me, only this time I refrained from expressing it. "It's just cute when you get all worked up."

She spun around to face me, placing her hands on her hips, which only brought my attention to her tits. Of course she noticed immediately were my gaze had fallen and crossed her arms to hide them from my view.

"I just meant that if that should ever happen, I want you to know now while I'm here to say it that it'd be okay." She didn't look pleased that I'd decided to toss that in. "Okay, now that I've said it, I'm done. I won't bring it up again. Can we just go back to bed now?"

I carefully tugged on her arm and led her back to bed. Once we were both tucked beneath the covers, she turned her body toward mine and looked up at me. Through the darkness I could see the torn look of despair in her eyes.

"I don't want to talk about things like that. It feels wrong. Like in some way I've moved on even though you're still here, and that's something that at this point I don't think I could ever do."

I was gonna argue, assure her again that falling in love after I was gone would be okay, but the urge faded the moment she laid her head upon my chest. She snuggled in close, her arms wrapped around me like a blanket. Her cheek nuzzled me softly as if she were attempting to find the perfect spot, which I knew was the place where she could hear my heartbeat beneath her ear.

No one could ever know the things running through my mind, unless they themselves were living the same reality as I was. But my need to take care of everything now was powerful. I didn't want to leave anything unsolved or untouched.

I'd spend my days at work even though I'd cut back tremendously. I'd worked my ass off to get where I was. I'd pushed myself through school, focusing on my degree. Now looking back, spending my nights and days to get my license as a pharmacist seem almost wasted. It was time I could have spent with Sawyer, but instead I'd spent it on a license I no longer needed. Yet I still had to provide for my wife. I still had to make sure she was taken care of when I was gone. It seemed strange now, going into the pharmacy and being faced with all those patients I knew were battling things themselves. Only the way they looked at me now was so different.

But life had to go on.

I could feel myself fading though I did my best to fight the weakness. Still, the fight was getting harder every day.

I wasn't ready yet. I wasn't ready to let go.

CHAPTER 7

S*awyer*

MY OBSTETRICIAN KNEW THE SITUATION AND I WAS so grateful for the efforts of her and her staff. I knew each time we went in for a visit, they'd spend just a little more time with us to allow us to hear the heartbeat of our child. They'd even sneak in an extra sonogram just because they could.

They did everything they could to involve Patrick as much as possible. Each visit was bittersweet for us. Though I tried hard each time to hide my sadness, it was impossible.

Like today.

Tears pooled in his eyes as he stared up in joy at the screen before us, and when they slowly crept along his cheeks, he did absolutely nothing to wipe them away.

"Everything looks really good," Dr. Haynes said as she

held still, capturing our baby's heartbeat. "Very strong heartbeat, and you're measuring at about fourteen weeks now."

She took a couple images and printed them out, then handed them to Patrick with a look on her face that I could only describe as heartbreak. My own tears fell then, and I closed my eyes for a moment and silently prayed that he would at least get the chance to see our baby. Maybe get the chance to hold him or her and know them. God, I wanted that so badly.

When I opened my eyes, Patrick and the doctor were looking at me. She seemed confused at how I'd zoned out for a moment, but Pat wasn't. It was like he knew what thoughts and wishes were rolling around in my mind. Ten to one, he wished the same thing.

We walked toward his truck in silence, holding hands. If he was feeling anything close to what I was, I knew he felt that rawness too.

After he helped me up into the truck, he closed the door and walked around to his side, which took a little more effort for him than it had a month ago.

It was heartbreaking watching the man who had always seemed invincible struggle now. But he was so stubborn, so proud. I knew he wouldn't admit he needed help.

As he closed the door, he looked over at me with that same tortured expression. "I had copies of our wedding video made," he said, completely confusing me for a moment. "Gage also combined all the videos he and his parents had of him and me growing up. I put them with my own and what my mother could find too. I had everything put on a disc with two spare copies."

His reason was clear to me now.

"I want 'em to know me," he whispered, and damn it, I broke. "I want to be there even though I can't be, ya know?" I nodded because I couldn't speak.

He leaned in and took me in his arms, and for a moment we just stayed there, holding one another, saying nothing. Burying my nose against his chest, I breathed in his scent. I'd say I wanted to etch it into my memory, but I'd done that long ago. I could pick out that warm, musky scent of his anywhere. It was something I would never forget.

"You remember that place we went to the summer before we got married?" I leaned back as he kept hold of my hands. "The Jack Warner, that place on Lake Tuscaloosa?"

"Yeah." Of course I remembered. We spent four days there, making love in the afternoon, taking walks at sunset. It was secluded and romantic.

"What would you say if I told you I booked us an extended weekend there?"

Part of me wanted to say, "No, we need to stay home where you can rest, not go walking through the woods or staying up to listen to a band playing on the back patio of some bed and breakfast." Instead, I went with what was playing in my heart on repeat. "I'd say that sounds amazing. I think we could use a little getaway."

"Four weeks from now." He squared his shoulders.

It was as if he was setting a goal, as if four weeks was nothing. The problem was, four weeks to us was like a lifetime. But I smiled, forcing myself to believe that four weeks was a piece of cake.

"It'll be like a small celebration for us, because by then we'll know what we're having." He looked down at my stomach and a grin tugged at the corner of his lips. "Though I already know it's a girl."

A week ago he'd brought home a pink teddy bear. On that same day, after I'd taken a trip to the store, I'd chosen a blue monkey. That night we laughed at our choices. Arguing over the baby's sex gave us something else to focus on.

"IT'S GOOD TO SEE HIM FINALLY ADMITTING THAT he needs to sleep too."

I smiled up at Gage as he entered the kitchen and offered my shoulder a gentle squeeze. It was midday and he'd come to spend the afternoon with Patrick. With fall slowly fading and winter rolling in, it was time for football season, and the game was one of many things they shared a love for. I'd heard so many stories of their years of playing ball together.

But one hour into the game, Pat had fallen asleep on the couch.

"He was never one for naps, you know that."

"Yeah." Gage moved toward the coffeepot on the counter and poured himself a cup before joining me at the table. Gage was at home here; he always had been. "When's the next appointment?"

"Tuesday."

The date on the calendar tortured me each time I looked at it. On that day we would once again be forced to face the fact that there was absolutely nothing we could do to extend our time together. It was the dreaded day that I would once again see the disease that was draining the life out of my husband.

"He said he went in for scans Friday."

I nodded and again silence fell between us. I hated the silence. It was where all my nightmares lay.

"I don't wanna overstep, but—" He took in a deep breath that caused me to look in his direction. "If you ever need me to go along, just know that I'm here. Just ask."

It was then that I really looked at Gage and noticed how exhausted he was too. He had dark stubble along his jaw and chin when he was usually so clean-shaven, and his hair hadn't been cut for a while when it was almost always perfectly trimmed. I had a feeling that was more Honor's taste than his own.

"You look worn out."

He chuckled and lifted his coffee cup to his lips. "Is that your way of telling me I look like shit, Sawyer?" He covered his smile with his cup as he took a drink before lowering the cup once more.

"I'm just saying that though I really appreciate the offer, and your help throughout this last couple months, you need to take care of you too."

"Just like you need to take care of you."

"I am," I assured him, though he didn't look convinced. Gage was a lot like Pat, and I knew I'd lose the fight if I dragged this out, so I moved on.

"I'm just saying I'm sure Honor would like you home too. That you have things that need to get done, a life to live."

Something flashed in his eyes, annoyance maybe. "Believe me, she's not at home waiting, Sawyer."

I knew I shouldn't push, but lately I found I was always desperate for something to focus on that wasn't Pat's next appointment. "Is everything okay?"

"Yeah, it's fine." He looked away from me.

"If you were Pinocchio, your nose would be growing at this very moment." My comment made him laugh and my own soft laughter joined his. It felt good.

"Let's just say without going into too much detail that my basement has become my bedroom."

My laughter died and I felt like an asshole for not thinking he could be having problems of his own during this time. I tended to forget that my problems weren't the only ones that existed, especially because mine felt like mountains compared to hills right now.

"I'm sorry."

"What are you sorry for? You didn't tell me to marry a

selfish woman. That's on me." Silence fell again because truthfully I had no idea what to say. "You know she actually told me that spending all my time here with Pat wouldn't change the outcome."

My stomach tensed with anxiety and irritation.

"She said I had a life to live and that one day I'd have to accept that I'd be living it without him." He still wouldn't look at me, and I was thankful because if he did, I was sure he'd notice my murderous expression. I always knew his wife was a bitch, but this was solid proof of her inability to feel anything for anyone but herself.

"She's supposed to support me, right? Be there for me if I'm having a tough time and comfort me." I didn't know if he was truly asking me or simply confirming what he already knew to be true. "She's too busy worrying about me painting her kitchen the ugliest fucking shade of green I've ever seen in my life before her friends come over at the end of the month. Our house is this month's gathering place, and that's all she can talk about. Not the fact I'm losing someone who's like a brother to me. It's like she doesn't care."

Because she doesn't. I didn't say it because I knew I didn't need to.

"This entire thing's just made me see that much clearer what I already knew. But enough about me." He smiled in that silly way he did when he was attempting to get himself out of an uncomfortable situation. Sometimes I felt as if I knew him as well as I did Patrick. They'd always been a package deal, as if by marrying Pat I adopted another big, muscle-bound goofball too.

"You deserve someone that'll stand by you no matter what," I said.

Gage was good man, and the fact Honor couldn't see that was enraging.

CHAPTER 8

P*atrick*

I WOKE WITH A FEELING OF DREAD. I KNEW WHAT was to come, and I'd rather skip right over the day. Being reminded of my doom just felt pointless. Sawyer and I would be better off without having to face the fact that I would miss so much and that she would be alone.

"I was just coming to wake you." I looked up at our open bedroom door to find Sawyer standing there. Her sweater pushed out at her waist over that sweet little bump that was now hard to hide. I loved seeing her body change. Knowing she'd still have a little part of me with her when I was gone gave me some joy throughout the heartache.

"You get more beautiful every day, you know that?" Her cheeks reddened as they always did when I gave her a compliment. "Come here."

She moved across the room and sat near me on the edge of the bed. I placed my hand over our child, and she placed hers over mine. I found that we did this often.

"Can you do something for me?"

"Anything." She smiled, and fuck, I felt it so deep in my stomach that my heart rate sped. With her by my side, I've never had a time when I didn't feel like the luckiest man alive.

I waited to speak the words I wanted to, just for a moment. Because I knew the second I did, her smile would fade and I wanted it to last just a bit longer.

"I don't want you to go today." She tensed as the smile slowly left her face, just as I'd thought it would. "I love you so much, Sawyer, and we both already know what he's gonna say. And I don't think I can take seeing that look on your face all over again."

"I'll be strong," she assured me, though I could already see the tears in her eyes.

"I know you will, baby." There was no doubt in my mind she would be; Sawyer was amazing. "But I already asked Gage to go with me."

"But I—"

"I need this, Sawyer." I felt like an asshole for shutting her out, but in a way I also felt like I was protecting her. We both knew I was fucking dying—hell, everyone did. I didn't need her to fall apart all over again when the doctor reiterated that. "Can you do this for me, please?"

Hesitantly she nodded, and I sat up and moved closer to her.

"I don't want days of sadness after a recap of all the things we heard a couple months ago." I'd put off going long enough already; I was only going today because she wanted me to. "My mother and Rachel are coming over." She narrowed her eyes as if realizing I'd had this all planned out without talking to her first. "They promised to make a feast fit for a king, and then tonight everyone will be here to enjoy it with us."

I knew her argumentative nature well enough to know she was pissed. Her nostrils flared, her lips pressed in a tight line, and her forehead wrinkled.

"Can I have a kiss?" I asked, tilting my head to get a better look at her. Her own head hung low as she fought a smile. "Or are you contemplating slugging me instead?"

Her shoulders shook slightly with laughter, and I knew then I was safe to move in closer.

"Kiss me." She lifted her head and stared at me. "Please."

She closed the distance between us, and the moment her lips touched mine, the stress of the last day lifted. I'd been trying to figure out the best way to break the news, and of course there was no good way. Which was the reason I waited until the morning of the appointment to tell her.

"I love you," I whispered just as she leaned in and stole one more kiss before moving back.

"I love you too." With her thumb she traced the line of my jaw, and my eyes involuntarily fluttered shut. "That will never change."

"HOW ARE YOU FEELING, PATRICK?" DR. SHEPPARD leaned back in his chair across from me and Gage. My file was opened before him, and those dreaded images of my fate were pinned to the board behind him—the x-ray that showed the aggressive monster inside me. "And don't say fine."

I chuckled, still feeling as if maybe I should have left Gage at home too. I could practically feel him staring a hole into the side of my head.

"You may be able to hide shit from Sawyer, but I can see

right through you." I looked to my right and locked eyes with Gage as he spoke. "So answer the doc's questions truthfully."

He was a cocky son of a bitch and he knew it.

"I feel like hell," I said, still staring at my best friend instead of my doctor. "But you know what hurts the most?" Gage held my stare without even a blink. "My fucking heart, man, because every day I watch my sweet wife fake being happy, though I know on the inside she's falling apart." He flinched. "I can take that each time I eat, I end up feeling sick. I can take the constant headaches and fatigue. It's that look on her face I can't accept. It pisses me off that I can't make it go away."

Silence settled over the room as Gage and I continued to stare at one another. I knew lashing out at him was wrong, but he was the only person who'd take it without growing angry. I had so much hate inside me that I'd attempted to bury, yet the only thing that did was make it worse.

"Have you been taking the pain medication regularly as prescribed?"

"Yes," I said without looking up at the doctor. Instead, I stared at the flat surface of the desktop that separated the two of us.

"Are you sure you don't want to consider chemotherapy?"

"'Run the risk of getting an infection that could potentially lead to my death or speed up the process," I said sarcastically. "Suffer from nausea, vomiting, and fatigue worse than I do already. And let's not forget the possibility of mouth sores, and maybe even memory loss. I think I'll pass. I want to be able to kiss my wife and love her the best way I can until my last day without all of that shit dragging me down."

I know Sawyer wanted me to try, but she wanted it for all the wrong reasons. I think somewhere deep inside, she allowed herself to actually believe that a miracle would somehow fix me. But the fact remained that nothing would fix what I have.

"So be honest with me, Doc," I said, finally lifting my gaze to meet his. "Will I make it to the birth of my child?"

CHAPTER 9

S awyer

I DIDN'T LIKE NOT KNOWING WHAT THE DOCTOR
had said. I didn't like the fact Gage and Patrick acted as if
they'd gone out for beers instead of sitting in an oncologist's
office. I'd pushed for two days now to find out what went on,
and the only thing I got was the brush-off.

They'd told me there was nothing new and no change in
Pat's condition, but I knew they were lying. I'd caught Gage
staring at Patrick more than once as if lost in deep thought,
and the more I watched it, the angrier I got.

I stood at the sink as they sat at the table behind me
while I washed the same plate again and again. I could hear
them talking and chuckling as if nothing was going on. The
longer I stood there, the more frustrated I got, until I
dropped the plate in the dishwater and turned to face them.

They continued to talk, not noticing me at first, but then

Gage glanced over at me and a blank look crossed his features.

"I know you both are lying," I said before turning to Patrick. "I also know that you didn't want me there because you didn't want me to hear that things may have gotten worse. And I know that you're aware how I sometimes still allow myself to believe you'll get better."

Patrick took a deep breath as he closed his eyes for a few seconds, then opened them again and met mine.

"But the both of you sitting there as if the visit didn't even take place isn't helping me any more than hearing what the doctor said myself." I was fully aware I was begging, but I didn't care. "So please, just tell me the truth."

Gage sat there frozen as if he didn't know whether he should stay or go. When he began to stand, Patrick told him to sit without taking his eyes off me.

"I'm not gonna get better, Sawyer."

That simple, direct statement hurt like hell, but I tucked it away without shedding a tear.

"I don't think I have to tell you that today I feel a little weaker than I did yesterday. I also know I don't have to tell you that tomorrow I'll feel even worse. I can either accept this thing and live with it for as long as I can, or I can let it drown me. I don't know about you, but I don't want to spend every day talking about what tomorrow may bring. I want to live in the now." I swallowed past the lump in my throat. "I told you from the beginning that I refused to let this illness to consume my mind, because it has already consumed my body."

Patrick stood from the table, bracing his hands on the edge. "Can we stop living in the dreaded future and start living in the present? Please, Sawyer, the last thing I want is to waste the time I have left with you on shit like this."

He didn't even wait for me to answer before he pushed off

the table and turned to leave the room. I stood there watching him go and feeling blindsided, though I'd caused it all myself.

"I get it." Gage's husky voice penetrated the silence, making my heart jump in surprise, and I met his stare. "How needing to know feels almost more important than taking your next breath. If I was in that position, the unknown would be torture."

I nodded, because it was exactly that.

"But after going with him to the doctor, hearing the fear from his side, I can see it differently now." I looked down at his hands, which were fisted together before him on the tabletop. "He's faced that he may not have a tomorrow, so living for today is his form of acceptance. You want my honest opinion?"

Again I nodded.

"Give him that. Let him see you laugh, and save your tears, Sawyer. Hell, give them to me if that'll help. But live every moment with him for the memories they'll provide you later. I don't know about you, but if I had the chance to make memories that would last me a lifetime, I'd want the happy ones and not those that would make me regret wasting valuable time on arguments."

I had to admit his words made sense.

"I'm gonna head out." Gage stood and moved toward me, where he placed his hand on my forearm. "If you need anything, either of you, please don't hesitate to call."

He leaned forward, and before I had time to register what he was doing, he placed a kiss to my forehead. "He needs us to be strong for him."

Without any further hesitation he stepped back and headed out the back door just off the kitchen.

I don't know how long I stood there letting his words roll

around in my mind. I felt as if I was in a trance, trapped between what I wanted to do versus what I needed to do.

"Did he leave?" My body jerked in surprise as Patrick stepped into the kitchen. I nodded as he moved closer and paused with only a few feet between us. "I'm sorry," His words hit me hard, and I moved forward and wrapped my arms around him, holding him tight.

"No," I said, my voice shaky and strained. "I'm sorry. It's just hard to face that there's nothing I can do."

"I know," he confessed as he held me tighter. "Believe me, sweetheart, I know."

It wasn't an easy choice, but I decided to give him what he needed most. I'd give him my laughter and days of happiness. I'd save the heartache for my moments alone, when I could blame them on a sappy movie, or when I found myself alone and with plenty of time to hide the evidence of my tears before he'd notice.

I'd fill every moment we were gifted with another memory I could treasure.

CHAPTER 10

P *atrick*

"Does she know you're doing this?" Gage held the two-by-four up while I used the nail gun to secure it.

"She will," I said with a chuckle as I anchored it to the wall with one last nail. "I always told her I was gonna make this room into the most gorgeous nursery. The thing about Sawyer...." I paused for a moment, because damn, even after all this time together, she still made my heart race when I thought of her. "She dreams big, Gage. She hides behind her fear now, but after we bought this place, she used to look through those magazines that had decoration shit. She'd circle things, and a few times I caught her cutting pictures out of them and putting them in this little container above the sink."

Gage grabbed for the second board and put it against the wall so I could drive the nails through it too. Holding the weight of the boards in place as I secured them wasn't as easy now as it once was.

"I want her to have that nursery," I confessed, feeling determined. "I want to know that she'll have that dream. That she'll be able to sit here in this little nook and read to our child while looking out over our backyard." I pointed toward the window. "It was that view that made us buy this place to begin with. I like to think that even though I won't be here, if the two of them can sit in this spot, they'll still feel like I am."

"They will," he assured me with a nod. "After we're done, this place will look like it belongs in one of those home magazines."

I'd never really been the kind of man who shares his heavy feelings with another man, or anyone for that matter. Whenever I got together with the boys, we'd always just hassle each other and rib each other, choosing to ignore what was truly on our minds. We left the feeling shit for the women. But lately I'd become that guy who says what he feels when he feels it because I may not have tomorrow.

"I know I've been asking a lot of you, Gage, but…." I took a deep breath, then looked up to meet his stare.

"I've told you that no matter what it is, I got you."

I knew he did, but I also knew he had his own shit to deal with, yet here he was with me. "If something happens and I don't get to finish this—"

"You will." He gave me a determined look, showing me that he believed this in his heart.

"But just in case, will you promise me that you'll do whatever it takes to get it done for her?"

"You have my word."

If I knew one thing, it was that Gage's word was his honor. The man was the most honest guy I knew. His heart was so full of love and dedication that I found myself wondering every day how Honor landed him. Yeah, she was fun to look at, and when you're young I guess things like that are appealing. I just always knew she wasn't a lifer. She was selfish and demanding.

"How're things going at home?" When he hung his head, I regretted bringing it up, until his shoulders shook with humor. "That good, huh?"

"She's insane." He finally looked up at me. I only arched my brow, wondering if he truly thought I would argue. I knew she was certifiable, though. "If you even think about saying, 'I told you so,' we're gonna have ourselves a few rounds right here, right now."

I held up my hands and chuckled. "No need for me to tell you something you already know." I leaned back against the doorframe and crossed my arms over my chest, waiting for him to continue.

"Last night I woke up to her standing over me, holding a basket of clothes. Before I could ask what the hell she was doing, she tipped the damn thing over on me, spouting off something about washing my own smelly laundry." I listened on, even though my chest shook with laughter. "What the bitch didn't know was that those clothes were already fucking clean."

"You still sleeping in the basement?"

"Yeah, and I can't remember ever sleeping so soundly." His expression was as deadpan as his tone. "I don't know what the hell I was thinking all those years ago. I think I even knew then that Honor wasn't the marrying type. She doesn't give a shit about anything but herself. Heartless, spoiled woman."

"But you love her?" Yes, I had to ask, because for as long as I could remember, Gage and Honor had seemed like two separate entities and not a unit.

"I think at one time I did, or maybe it was more lust then.

Who knows?" He paused a moment, as if thinking over some deep thought. "When I wake up and start my day, I should be happy to know she's my wife. I should want to run to her when something great happens or lean on her when I just need someone to listen, but I don't. It takes everything I have to force myself to go home at night. I think the only reason I do is because I don't trust that she wouldn't toss my shit out on the street."

"You know you can stay here." I'd offered before and so had Sawyer, yet he always declined.

"Though I appreciate it, I just need to find an apartment or something small."

"So it's happening?"

He looked over at me. "If by *it* you mean divorce, then yeah, it's happening. I already talked to my attorney, Pete, and got things moving. I just need to move out before they serve the papers because I wouldn't put it past her to slit my throat in the middle of the night."

"Don't you think she'll see it coming?"

"No," he said with a chuckle. "The woman actually thinks she has me over a barrel. She told Stacia that before long she'll have me whipped into the man she needs."

"What the fuck?"

"Yeah, Stacia went home and told Mark, then that ass came into the station with a bag of rawhides last week." I tried to hold back the fact I found that to be funny as hell, but I couldn't. "Yeah, yeah, laugh it up. But now every other firefighter at the station calls out to me and whistles to me like I'm a dog. The chief even brought in a bowl and set it on the floor in the common room. Assholes are loving it a little too much if you ask me."

I laughed even harder as I slumped back against the wall, leaning over to clench my stomach with one hand.

It felt damn good to laugh, even though it was at the

expense of my buddy, but I knew he didn't mind. Because seeing me laugh like this was rare these days.

"Go right ahead." I looked up, tears pooling in my eyes as he shook his head, attempting to hide his own smile, but it was too late. I'd seen it.

"I could get you a cozy fleece bed," I said as I straightened up. "Set it out right in front of the fire. I hear dogs love that kinda shit."

"Eat it up, you dick." He turned back to focus on the task at hand. "I'm gonna have all my calls from her forwarded straight to your phone."

"That woman doesn't scare me." I waved him off as I moved in with the nail gun. "Now Sawyer, on the other hand, she scares me when she gets angry."

"Sawyer's too sweet to be mean."

I paused with the gun pressed to the board overhead and gave him a direct stare. "Believe me when I say she has a mean streak in her. I've just learned to avoid it."

He still didn't look convinced, but it was true. Sawyer was a sweetheart, but she could bring the ring of fire too. Though I always wanna laugh when she's pissed because she's too damn cute, I learned the hard way not to.

CHAPTER 11

S *awyer*

"ARE YOU BOTH READY?"

Patrick squeezed my hand firmly in his, and a big smile spread over his face. "So ready," he said with a gleam in his eyes.

I turned back to face the doctor and nodded, and she grabbed the tube of gel.

"You know the drill," she said as she tipped it upside down and the warm liquid pooled on my abdomen.

Pure excitement hit me, the kind that was so uncontrollable it made me feel like flying. I watched her closely, shaking with anticipation. In my mind, I was screaming, "Please hurry," because it felt like she was moving in slow motion.

Closing my eyes tight just as she pressed the transducer

against me, I heard the swooshing sound fill the silence. Patrick's grip tightened on my hand.

"We have a hand." I opened my eyes as the doctor moved the wand over me, doing her best to capture everything she could. "A shoulder, and here we have—" Our baby shifted. "—a leg."

I looked at Patrick to find his gaze practically glued to the monitor. I could simply watch him watching the screen and get the most out of this experience we were sharing.

"We've got us a stubborn one," Dr. Haynes added with a laugh.

"Just like Momma," Pat said with a smirk, making the doctor laugh, but he still didn't look away.

"But if I can move 'em just a little, we might be able to see the sex."

My heart rate sped as I squinted at the screen. I think I may have even held my breath, hoping she could see what she needed to.

"We do want to know, right?" she asked.

"Yes," Patrick answered so quickly that Dr. Haynes beamed again.

"Whose' guess is what?"

"Girl." Again Patrick didn't even pause.

"Boy," I said, nudging him with our joined hands, and he looked away from the screen just long enough to toss me a wink before focusing once again on our child.

"Well, it looks like...." She paused just to torment us, I think. And it was working because his grip tightened again almost to the point of hurting, and I wiggled my head, getting him to let up. "Daddy is right."

"It's a girl," Patrick whispered as he let go of my hand and stood.

"Sure is," Dr. Haynes confirmed and Patrick let out a little laugh. I wasn't even sure if he realized he'd done it.

Then he looked at me, tears pooling in his eyes and leaned forward, taking my face in his hands. "I told you we were having a girl."

I laughed. Normally that cocky, I-am-the-king attitude would've triggered a round of banter between us, but I let him have this moment. His lips pressed against mine and a little chuckle escaped him. "I'm rarely wrong, babe. You should know this by now."

We left the doctor's office feeling high on life. For now, the fact we were having a daughter overruled thoughts of what we were facing. The smiles on our faces were so bright and deep that I felt nothing could bring us down at the moment.

Patrick spun around and stepped in front of me, hooking my waist and pulling me close. "Let's do something we haven't done in a long time."

"What? Get frisky in the cab of your truck?" I wagged my brows suggestively and he chuckled as if he didn't have a worry in the world. That alone gave me such a rush of joy it brought tears to my eyes. "I'm just saying"—I shrugged—"we haven't done that in a while."

"No, we have not," he agreed, leaning in to press a kiss to my lips. "In fact, I think that is a great idea, only not in the parking lot of your obstetrician's office."

"Where's your sense of adventure?"

"Oh I'm adventurous," he said while cupping my ass and moving me toward his truck only a few feet away. "Are you taunting me?"

I tried to answer him, but couldn't at the moment. With his current assault on my neck, and the way he was pushing his growing erection against me, I lost my train of thought.

"Maybe I should remind you that I don't normally back down from a dare." My back bumped against the cool metal of his truck and he pushed his body against mine a little harder. "If you're not scared of the consequences of being caught, then neither am I."

The sound of a car door shutting only a few feet away didn't faze him, yet it reminded me that we were, in fact, in a parking lot. Then the reality of what I'd started hit me and I laughed.

"I can see the headlines now." I allowed my head to rest back against the door of his truck. "'Couple caught with their pants down in local obstetrician's parking lot.'"

"I don't have to pull mine down, though. At least not all the way."

"Maybe we should save the public sex for another day?"

He arched a brow but kept me in place with his body. "Now where is *your* sense of adventure?"

I loved the gleam in his eyes. We'd both forgotten that fun-loving playfulness lately. That would be one of the things I'd miss the most after he was gone. Things had always been so easy for Patrick and me. We'd had hard times, but there was always that intense bond between us, one that only the greatest of friends turned lovers could share. He could make me smile even when it was last thing I wanted. It was like he could dig deep through all the heaviness inside me and find that ember of heat and reignite the fire within me.

"You're my adventure." I cupped his face in my hands and looked at him with all the intensity I felt. "Our life, our journey, it's all my adventure."

I could see the impact my words had on him in the shining gleam of unshed tears in his eyes and the way he pressed his lips tightly together.

Though some would think that was just some cheesy line, it held such depth to us. Every single struggle we'd faced, every obstacle we'd been forced to overcome was all part our fate. I knew then that I'd been given the gift of this man to show me that I was, in fact, strong.

I'd spent my life prior to meeting Patrick feeling as if I had no great purpose. I struggled to find my way, but then by chance I crossed paths with this man and he showed me such a great love—a love I was sure I would never find again but was blessed to have now, if only for a short time more.

I would teach our child that love. That was my purpose. I had to believe that. That I was here to instill that same love in our daughter; our little girl who was created through such a powerful connection that even our impending doom couldn't penetrate it.

"As you are mine," he whispered just before kissing me once more, and in that single kiss I felt everything he couldn't say. It brought me a strange sense of peace, because I knew that even if we didn't have tomorrow, this moment would forever be etched in my mind.

It was *ours*.

CHAPTER 12

P*atrick*

THIS LITTLE GETAWAY WE'D PLANNED WOULD BE good for us. It would give us some time to enjoy one another without everything we'd been forced to face weighing us down. I could see the excitement in Sawyer's eyes when we pulled up to the front doors of The Jack Warner Retreat. Her face lit up when the young woman behind the counter mentioned the honeymoon suite as she passed us the key card.

I wanted her to remember this trip. It would most likely be our last one together, and though the idea of that was fucking painful, I didn't let it take away from my joy at having this time away. I didn't let the headaches and nausea I'd had for the last couple days take away from it, either.

This was *our* time and we would enjoy it no matter what.

I stepped into the room after her and lowered the bag to the floor as she looked around in awe.

"Do we really need all this space?" she asked, still smiling.

I wrapped my arms around her middle and rested my hands over the bump that held our child. "I want this to be perfect."

She leaned back against me, arching her neck just enough to press a kiss to my jawline. "Being here with you already makes it perfect."

Closing my eyes, I just held her close for a few moments. Over the last few days, I'd felt my body slowly losing strength and exhaustion creeping in, along with the terror. The idea that my life and my time with those I love was coming to an end was overpowering. I knew that this would haunt her too. I also knew I had to hold it together for her.

But the fear of being without her was still there. At times it was so fucking powerful, I felt like I was drowning in it.

I was not a man of faith, but these days I wished I was. I found myself praying so often that I felt guilty for reaching out only when I was so afraid. I wanted to know I'd see her again after I was gone. I wanted to believe I'd get the chance to hold her and feel her love again. The idea that when I was gone, I was gone forever was terrifying. Sawyer had been part of me since the day we met. Like the missing piece I hadn't known was missing until I stumbled upon it.

I was pulled from my thoughts when her body turned within my hold. Resting her palms against my chest, she looked up at me with the sweetest smile. "So what would you like to do first, Mr. Cooper?"

I didn't miss the way she bit her lower lip as she tried to hide her smile. She slid her hands to my shoulders so she could step closer and press her tits firmly to my chest. "We could take a walk," she said with a sweep of her tongue over her lip. "Or we could go down and have an early lunch."

"Lunch sounds good," I replied, taking a step toward the center of the room, moving her body with my own. "But only after we mess up the sheets over there."

"That sounds perfect." She hooked the back of my neck and pulled me in closer. "Better than perfect."

Our lips connected in a slow, tantalizing kiss.

Words faded as the hunger that was always present between us took over as our hands began to speak for us, showing one another just how much we craved each other's touch.

Carefully and very lovingly I lowered her to the bed and crawled in after her, bringing my body to hers once more. So much emotion ran through me as she looked up at me with that you-are-my-hero expression. Fuck, it used to make me feel so powerful. Now it just made me feel like I was failing her. I'd made a promise to protect her forever, and now that ability was being forcefully taken from me.

If I spoke now, I knew I'd break. The ache was so real, I felt like I had hot coals buried deep in my chest. Sawyer was the one person for me, and even though I wouldn't be able to grow old with her as I'd planned, I'd at least been given the chance to experience what a love like ours felt like.

***

"Do you think we should grab dinner?" Sawyer's voice was muffled against my chest. I held her to me, tighter than I probably should, but I didn't want to let her go. "We missed lunch," she added with a giggle.

"Are you complaining?"

"Absolutely not. But I'm pregnant and that means food is a bit necessary now."

"Yeah," I said as I slowly and begrudgingly released my hold on her. "I guess I should feed you, huh?"

"Food, and maybe a little walk to bring some life back to my legs." I arched a brow because a man loved to hear that after spending the last few hours holding his wife hostage in bed. "You liked that a little too much. I can see the pride rolling off you in waves."

"Information like that is good for a man's ego."

I moved in for a kiss and she gripped my face. "You and I both know that if I allow you to kiss me, we'll most likely be missing dinner too."

I leaned toward her a little more just to taunt her and she turned her face away from me and laughed into her pillow. "Okay, food and then a walk," I assured her, loving the sound of her laughter. "Then it's back here for a shower, and then we climb back into this bed and go to sleep."

"Deal," she said, though I could tell she didn't trust that I was being truthful.

"Breakfast in bed tomorrow," I added, gaining an even bigger smile. "Let's move, woman. Are you trying to starve me or what?"

I hurried out of bed, smiling as her laughter filled the room. Exhaustion made me move a little slower than I wanted, but I did my best to hide it.

CHAPTER 13

S *awyer*

I SAT ON THE PRIVATE DECK JUST OFF THE BACK OF our suite, wrapped in a fleece blanket as I waited for sunrise. The last few days had been amazing. We spent our days dining and exploring the trails near the lodge that gave us a clearer picture of the land surrounding it, and our afternoons making love before falling asleep in one another's arms.

But I could tell Patrick was hiding his fatigue, and God, it worried me. He needed sleep and quiet instead of running around all day. I felt like he was doing this for me, and of course that only made me feel even guiltier. But instead of telling him this trip hadn't been the best idea, I pretended I didn't see the circles under his eyes growing darker or how he struggled to get out of bed. He needed me to live in the moment; he was desperate for me to.

Yet when he was asleep and I could let myself feel, I faced

the fact that our time was running short. I was watching the man I love fade before me while pretending everything was okay, and I was slowly falling apart.

With tears streaming down my cheeks, I lifted my phone to my ear and closed my eyes as it rang.

"Sawyer?"

"Yeah, it's me."

"Is everything okay?" I heard the fear in Gage's question.

"Yes. He's sleeping," I assured him.

Silence settled over us and I regretted calling him.

"What is it?"

"Do you remember that night in the kitchen," I went on, "when you said I should only let him see me laugh and to save the tears?"

Gage took a deep breath and let it out slowly. "Yeah, Sawyer, I remember."

"Do you remember what else you said?"

"I told you to give them to me if it helps."

The moment he told me what I needed to hear, I began to cry quiet tears, yet I knew he could sense them.

"I wasn't lying when I said I was here, not just for him but for you too," Gage said, and I covered my mouth to muffle my sobs. "You see it, too, don't you?"

"The way he's fading before us? Yes."

"It's hard to watch," I confessed in a whisper.

"Harder than anything I've ever been forced to go through." I nodded as if Gage could see it. "I sometimes find myself imagining what life will be like without him. What I'll do without having him here to push me. Life and its meaning just seems pointless sometimes without him, you know?"

"I do." I'd had those same thoughts often.

"But then I remember something he told me while we were working on that damned fence." Gage paused, as if making sure I was paying full attention. "He said that he may have only had a short time here, but in that time he feels like he's been gifted with more than enough. Like he was the luckiest guy in the world for being granted the little time he had with the greatest of people." The fact Gage was now crying broke me even more. "He told me to live, Sawyer. He told me to stop sitting around waiting for something great and just go find it."

"That's good advice." Gage had a bad habit of settling for the mediocre as long as those around him were happy.

"Yeah," he said, and I sensed him smiling. "That husband of yours is pretty great."

"Yes, he is. The greatest." I took a deep breath, doing my best to calm myself. "Thanks, Gage," I whispered, looking out over the trees as the sun peeked through the branches. "Thanks for being there when I needed to break."

"Anytime," he whispered. "I should thank you too."

We sat there in silence as the sounds of our breathing calmed us and reminded us that we weren't going through this alone.

"SAWYER? IS THAT YOU, BABE?""

I turned at the sound of his raspy voice. I'd just come inside after taking some time to pull myself together. The drapes were still shut, keeping the room dark. I wanted him to rest for as long as he could. "Yeah," I whispered as I moved toward the bed. "Did I wake you?"

"No," he assured me as I sat beside him on the edge of the bed. "What woke me was your absence." He cupped my thigh as if to hold me securely in place. "It's almost like my body knows when you aren't near."

"I know how that feels," I confessed, feeling that heavy

weight on my chest once again. "The only time I feel completely whole and at ease is when you're near."

His eyes closed for a few seconds as though he was fighting off a sad thought, before he opened them again. He took a deep breath and flinched.

"Are you feeling okay?" I asked.

"I'm good."

"You do realize just how well I know you, right?" Patrick gave me a puzzled look. "That with just one glance, I can sense when you're lying. So spare me from having to drag it out of you and just be honest with me now."

He stared back at me, like his silence would make me forget the question. When he realized I wouldn't falter, he looked away. "Just feeling a little queasy, is all."

"Queasiness doesn't make you flinch in pain, Patrick."

"Stubborn," he mumbled, still looking at the foot of the bed.

"Yes, you are," I said. "Where does it hurt?"

He didn't answer and I did my best to hide my irritation, but with each passing second it pushed at me harder.

"Don't ignore me, Pat." He finally met my gaze. "I've done as you've asked and focused on us and not so much on what's to come. But you can't ask me to ignore the fact you're in pain. That's being unfair."

Again I was met with silence.

"Where does it hurt?" I said slowly and directly.

His nostrils flared and he squinted in irritation.

"All over," he confessed, as if the words pained him. "Is that what you want to hear? That when I breathe it hurts, when I stand It's excruciating, and the simple act of making love to my wife takes everything I have inside of me?"

It was now my turn to fall silent.

"But I refuse to let this stop me from fucking living, Sawyer. I won't let it win, not until I have to."

Tears pricked my eyes and I did my best to hold them back.

"I love you. More than I could ever express." He sat up and reached out for me. "I can't tell you not to worry, because I know you will. Just trust me when I say that if it ever becomes too much, I'll tell you. But for now, I can't let go of my ability to live my life just yet."

I nodded even though my heart was screaming for me to fight him on this. But I knew fighting wouldn't accomplish anything.

"We have one more night here before we go back home," he whispered as he cupped my cheek. "I want us to spend it happy."

"Okay." I leaned in and pressed a kiss to his lips to hide the fear in my eyes. "But I'm exhausted, so I'd like nothing more than to curl up beside you and fall asleep in your arms."

I was nowhere near tired, but he needed rest.

"Climb on in here," he said just before lying back once more. "Place your head right here," he directed with his hand over his heart, and that heaviness in my chest grew so strong I feel like I couldn't breathe.

I buried my body beneath the covers and curled around his warmth. With my head rested just where he wanted it, I closed my eyes tight and willed the tears away. Doing my best to hide the emptiness consuming me, I concentrated on breathing evenly.

"Always loved you right like this," he confessed. "Your body so close to mine it feels like we're the same person."

I took deep breaths as I thought of all the reasons life was so damn unfair.

"Love burying my face in your hair, just breathing you in."

Those were the words most girls dreamed of hearing, and they made our love feel more solid and concrete. But hearing them now was like a slow form of torture, because they were tearing the small amount of control I had left to pieces.

"You were made just for me, Sawyer Cooper," he whispered sleepily. "I truly believe that."

I squeezed my eyes shut tighter as I curled into him closer.

"Forever my girl."

Tears rolled along my cheeks as I did all I could to wipe them away before he noticed. I was thankful sleep had taken him over and he was oblivious to the shattering of my soul.

CHAPTER 14

I was twenty-six weeks along today, and Patrick loved being able to feel our little girl move around inside me. I'd wake up in the middle of the night to him holding my stomach and whispering to her.

Sometimes I would just lie there and pretend to be asleep just to listen to him. He'd talk of times in her life where she may need a father and then apologize for not being here to share them with her. He told our sweet little one she should always turn to Uncle Gage, because if her daddy couldn't be here to protect her, there was no man he'd trust more to do it.

Those times were breath-stealing, and I was blessed to be a part of them. I'd be able to share these memories with my little girl when she was old enough to understand just how much her daddy loved her without even meeting her.

It was getting harder and harder to face each day. The possibility of Patrick being here to meet his daughter was beginning to look unlikely. He'd lost a lot of weight, and his strong arms, solid thighs, and overall muscle tone had begun to wilt. The man who had always seemed so strong and powerful had become weak and frail, and I was powerless to stop it.

He slept often, and I'd spend hours focusing on the rise and fall of his chest as if I needed to ensure he was still here with me. Morbid, maybe, but it was reassurance.

Since we'd returned home I watched him battle to accept that he could no longer do the things he'd been able to. It broke my heart to see him sitting back watching while his father and Gage worked on the nursery he was so adamant about completing. But his participation meant just as much to me because they were simply taking his vision for the room and making it a reality.

The hardest part was seeing his disappointment. I would never be able to get used to that defeated look on Patrick's face. He'd always been so confident, so driven. It was hard to keep him down under any circumstance.

But nothing about where we were now made my love for him any weaker. It only made me love him more. I admired him for needing to stay strong though he was fighting a constant war. He was trying to protect me from the sadness even though he was the one faced with such defeat.

He was my hero. He always would be.

I WOKE TO PATRICK MOANING IN HIS SLEEP. WITH each move his agony became more obvious.

"Pat," I whispered as I touched his shoulder. He jerked in surprise, his eyes wide as he looked around the room as if he didn't know where he was. "Honey, are you hurting?" The moment the words left my lips, I knew they were ridiculous. Of course he was hurting; he was always hurting.

"Yeah," he confessed. It was easier these days to get him to admit when he needed my help. At this point we were both past trying to protect the other. "Can you get my pills? Maybe a drink of water too?"

"I'll be right back."

I hurried to the kitchen and gathered his medication and a bottle of water before rushing back to our bedroom. Panic shot through me at the sight of the empty bed and I looked around the room.

"Patrick?"

Coughing and gagging came from the hallway and I moved toward it with growing unease. The sounds came from the small bathroom at the end.

Stepping into the doorway, I found him hunched over the toilet, his shoulders rising and falling as if he was attempting to catch his breath after a long run.

"I can't do this," he confessed with sadness. "I've tried, Sawyer. God I've tried. I just can't."

I wasn't sure if he was admitting defeat against tonight or life in general, but either possibility terrified me.

He turned his head just enough to look over at me and I swear my heart cracked when I saw his face glistening with fresh tears. "I've tried to fight through it, but the pain and exhaustion are becoming too much. I guess somehow I allowed myself to believe I was invincible. But, babe, I'm not. I need help."

I moved forward and knelt beside him. "I'm here, right here. Just tell me what I can do."

"You can't do anything, sweetheart. It's bigger than both of us."

I stared at him in confusion, then his words slammed into me.

"Hospital?"

When he nodded and began to push up off the floor, my heart sank as panic filled me. I couldn't do this alone.

My fear must have been written all over my face because I

could see the moment he registered it. His expression softened the way it always did when he felt the need to console me, which I found ironic. In his suffering he reached out for me and helped me stand, ensuring I felt the comfort of his touch.

"This is not me saying it's my time," he said slowly and with conviction. "I just need some help dealing with the pain."

I nodded, because frankly I couldn't speak. I had that deep fiery feeling in my chest that made my throat feel as if it had fused shut. With one hand linked with mine, he led us toward the bedroom and sat at the edge of the bed. He patted the space next to him, indicating I should join him as he reached for his phone.

I watched in silence as he dialed Gage's number and lifted the phone to his ear. "Hey, brother." There was a pause as Patrick's gaze met mine. "Not feeling the greatest. Do you think you can come pick up me and Sawyer?"

Through the silence that followed, I heard Gage murmuring on the other end of the line.

"We'll be ready."

He ended the call and wrapped his arm around my shoulders. I went willingly when he pulled me toward him.

"I've been researching names," Patrick whispered so lightly I almost missed it. "Trying to come up with something that has meaning."

I fisted his shirt, needing something to hold on to.

"Now, I know we're not Jewish, but I've found a Hebrew name that has the meaning I'd hoped for."

"What is it?" I would name our child almost anything if it held significance for him.

"Abigail," he said as if in awe of it. "It means 'father's joy.'" I closed my eyes tight, allowing a shaking breath to slowly escape. "Though I may not be here for her—"

"Please don't say that."

"I need to." I buried my face in his shirt as if that would drown out his words. "I may not be here, Sawyer, but I want her to know that even though I'm gone, she was her father's joy. She's a gift, not only for me, but for you. Because with her here, there will always be a little part of me with you too."

I had no hope of keeping it together at this point. My God, I ached so terribly I felt like I was being ripped apart slowly.

"Abigail Reese Cooper," he said, and I knew without a doubt he'd just named our daughter. Even if I'd hated it, the name would be hers. Reese was Patrick's middle name and nothing would honor him more than giving her yet another part of her father. Knowing he'd spent the time to carefully choose the arrangement meant the world.

"I love it." I meant it too. "She'll know every day of her life just how much her daddy loved her."

Patrick squeezed me just a little tighter and we waited in silence for Gage to arrive. The only sounds that could be heard were my sniffles as I tried my hardest to stay strong.

CHAPTER 15

I sat in the waiting room, staring at the large doors my husband was led through what felt like hours ago. I didn't like being left in the dark and wanted to be at his side, but I knew I couldn't get in the doctors' way.

The moment I heard my name I practically leaped from the chair and rushed toward the young nurse. Her eyes widened in surprise as she took a step back. "Mrs. Cooper?"

"Yeah, that's me," I said, eager to get to Patrick.

"Dr. Sheppard arrived a few moments ago and he's in with your husband now."

"I'd like to see him."

"Of course." She gave me a reassuring smile. "I've been directed to take you to the family waiting area just outside his room. Once the doctor is finished examining him, we'll take you to the room where he'll go over everything."

She looked to my left, and I followed her gaze.

Gage stood from his seat and shoved his hands deep in his pockets, looking almost as terrified as I felt. "He comes too," I said. "He's Patrick's brother and he'd want him in the room as well."

The nurse nodded, though I'm not sure she bought the brother excuse, but he was the closest thing to a brother Pat had. And Patrick would want him to hear what the doctor had to say so Gage could support us both.

Gage took a deep breath in and a slow release as if he was preparing himself for something he was dreading. We followed the nurse through those dreaded doors. The beeping of machines and the scurrying footsteps of doctors and nurses brought the reality of the situation front and center. I wasn't sure what the doctor would say, but I had a feeling that everything would change after tonight, more than it already had.

We waited in an area much smaller than the last. I swear I could feel the walls closing in on me with each passing second.

"You keep wiggling that way, you're gonna find yourself on the floor." I looked to my left and saw Gage smiling at me. He tapped my knee with his finger and chuckled. "Little girl's probably bouncing around in there wondering what the hell is going on."

I snickered at the thought and was thankful for having him here to keep me sane. If I didn't have Gage keeping me grounded, I would most likely be curled up in a ball sobbing uncontrollably with the fear of what was to come.

"Don't worry, she's paying me back by pushing on my bladder with fierce dedication."

When his forehead crinkled up and his face scrunched, I laughed.

The same nurse from earlier reappeared in the doorway and we looked up at her as if she were our lifeline.

"You two can follow me." She offered a supportive smile, and I wondered if that was part of their training. If they took a course on compassion and how to help families get through hardships. Granted, some nurses I've come across would have failed that course, but this one just had that sweetness about her.

"Thank you," I offered as we followed her to Patrick's room.

The moment I stepped inside, that familiar emptiness filled my chest. Seeing him in that hospital bed, looking as if he'd finally faced the fact he was weakening shattered me. I now realized why he'd wanted to keep me sheltered from it. My tears were so thick that my vision blurred.

"Hey, pretty girl." His voice was weak, raspy, and groggy, as if he'd just woken up. "Come over her and give me one of those kisses I love so much."

With each step I took toward him, I could feel myself falling apart, like pieces of me were being chiseled away to expose my bleeding heart. I wanted to ignore it and to forget that our time together was limited. I just wanted to pretend this was a nightmare and I would wake up to find him happy and healthy.

Only I knew that wasn't going to happen. That was clearer now than ever.

"Dry those eyes," he said as I reached the side of his bed. He linked our fingers, then pulled them to his lips. Seconds passed in silence. Then a long beep made me jump.

I looked around frantically as the nurse walked to the opposite side of the bed and began punching buttons on the machine next to it.

"You better slow that racing heart of yours." She placed her hand on his shoulder and gave it a gentle squeeze. I shifted my gaze back to meet his and found him smiling.

"Sorry," he whispered, "but whenever my gorgeous wife is near, that sorta happens."

The nurse smiled, the doctor shook his head, and Gage chuckled. My heart swelled, knowing that even while suffering, Patrick still needed to make those around him smile.

I leaned over and pressed my lips to his, giving him that kiss he'd asked for not that long ago. "You wipe that fear from your eyes," he said with conviction when I was close enough that only I could hear. "I'm not going anywhere yet, you hear me?"

"Now that the two of you are here, I'd like to go over the care plan Patrick and I have agreed to." I turned and Dr. Sheppard looked past me at my husband. "The pain medication I prescribed is no longer giving him the relief he needs. The cancer has progressed to the point that other forms of pain management need to be taken to offer him comfort."

I swallowed past the massive lump in my throat.

"Let's not forget the increase in his weight loss due to the vomiting and lack of appetite."

Tremendous weight loss, I thought, yet remained focused on the doctor.

"He has also expressed concerns about the onset of confusion and anxiety."

I turned to look at Pat, puzzled by this information. His need to keep things hidden shouldn't have surprised me; he'd spent so much time trying to keep my sadness at bay.

"I would like to admit him—" Patrick gave a displeased groan. "And by that reaction, I think it's safe to say the patient disagrees."

"Doesn't matter," Gage said, surprising us all. "He needs to be here, so he'll be here."

Patrick gave him a displeased look, but instead of running to the rescue of either man, I stood there silently as they battled it out.

"Since when did you become my dad?"

"I'm the guy who sat next to your wife for the last hour while she damn near shook herself out of her chair with worry." Even though I didn't look at Patrick, I knew he was watching me. "I also listened to you cry out in pain every time I hit a bump or took a turn on our drive here. So if this doctor thinks it's best that you stay here to get you the pain relief you need, then you'll stay. Because neither I nor your wife will be taking you home until this gentleman over here believes it's safe."

We were met with silence. I think it's safe to say we were all a bit taken aback at Gage's assertiveness. He was always such a "go with the flow, do whatever is easiest as long as you're happy" kind of guy.

"Any objections?" Gage asked. "That's what I thought," he said before anyone could complain or attempt to negotiate. "So, Doc, tell us more about this plan."

CHAPTER 16

"How's Grumpy Bear doing this morning?" When I looked up, the exhaustion and fear of the night hit me. Willow gave me a concerned look, kneeling before me. "Sawyer, did you get any sleep at all?"

"Some," I lied, and I knew she knew it. "Okay, very little."

"Why don't you go home, take a shower, maybe sneak in a nap?"

I looked over her shoulder and focused on Patrick. He looked so peaceful curled on his side, snoring lightly. Much different than he had the first night here, and the nights prior to that at home. Things were beginning to change rapidly. With each groan of agony from him, I felt like a part of me died a little.

Last night was his second one in the hospital, and it was terrifying and upsetting. They'd tried tramadol first and he grew agitated and angry almost immediately. That was heart-breaking to watch. Patrick wasn't a mean man, and I never wanted to see that side of him again.

"They started him on morphine," I said, ignoring her suggestion. "He seems like he's sleeping better, almost like he's feeling no pain. At least for the time being. I know that will change again when we least expect it to." Taking in a deep breath, I continued to stare at my husband.

"Dad said yesterday was rough." Willow took my hand. I nodded, not wanting to recap what he said or did on the tramadol. Each time I closed my eyes, I saw him sit up in his bed and look at me like I was the enemy.

"Leave."

That one word and the hateful glare he gave me had made me feel more broken than I ever had before.

"He didn't mean it, you know," Willow said, as if she could read my thoughts.

"I know." I did, but it didn't take the hurt away. Maybe hormones made his words affect me so much, but they stuck with me no matter how hard I attempted to forget them. "Just hard, that's all."

"You're exhausted." I looked back toward her but barely registered her face as I looked into her eyes. "Being here isn't helping."

"I can't leave him," I said. "I'm where I need to be."

When she realized I wasn't going to budge, she stood and sat in the chair beside me. For a few minutes we just watched Patrick sleep. Every so often he would twitch, and I would jerk in response as if we were wired together.

Gage left a few hours ago—feeling exhausted himself, I know—to get to the station for his shift. I knew he was reluctant to leave, but I assured him I'd call if anything changed. Last night, I'd watched Gage stare at Patrick while he slept. He was the first to rush to his side each time he showed any sign of discomfort.

"Patrick chose a name." My emotions were taking over, and at that point I just needed to talk. "It's beautiful, and the fact he spent so much time choosing it makes it even more special."

"Am I allowed to know?"

We hadn't talked about it, but I wanted everyone to know. "Abigail Reese." A tear ran over my cheek and dripped onto my arm as I closed my eyes briefly. "It means 'a father's joy.'"

When Willow didn't speak I looked at her and found that she, too, was fighting her emotions. She stared at her younger brother, and for the first time I saw the desolation in her eyes that I'd been feeling for days. Willow was always so strong and put-together and always seemed to have a solution for everything. But we were all realizing that nothing could fix what was taking place before us.

"Sometimes being strong is overrated," she finally said. "I believe all things happen for a reason, but I just can't see the reason for this. It's cruel, really, to bless him with such a great gift and then take him away before allowing him to experience it."

Willow was the backbone of their family, the "take no shit, keep everyone grounded" person. She always had an answer or explanation for everything. But seeing her so lost and unsure like this was like seeing a completely different person.

"I still remember the day I walked in at Mom and Dad's and found him standing in the kitchen wearing a smile that lit up the room." I closed my eyes as I tried to imagine that smile. "He told us he'd finally met the woman he'd marry one day."

I turned to look at her, which only caused her to smile.

"He talked about you almost as if you were an angel." Tears filled my eyes just as they've done so many times over the last few days, blurring my vision once again. "A girl with golden hair, the kindest eyes, and a smile that made him feel like he was floating. And that laugh." I wiped at the tears rolling along my cheeks. "He referred to it as the most beautiful song he'd ever heard."

"Why are you telling me this?" I sobbed as I leaned forward and placed my head in my hands.

"Because I wanted you to know that even though what he said yesterday made you feel a little lost, he didn't want that. Sawyer, my brother is so deeply in love with you it's almost unrealistic. A love that pure and untouchable can't be tainted by what he's going through."

I took in one deep breath after another, trying to regain my composure.

"It's gonna get harder, Sawyer."

"It's already hard," I whispered.

Willow placed her hand on my back and rubbed it in soothing circles. "There's gonna be times when that anger is gonna return. There will be times your heart will feel like it's breaking in half, and when it reaches that point, I want you to remember that story I just told you so you'll know that whatever he says isn't what he truly feels. Remember that you are the most important person to him and if he could control the future, we both know he'd never bring a dark moment upon you."

I nodded because I knew what she'd said was true.

"He adores you, Sawyer. He has from the moment he saw you stumbling across that parking lot toward him."

CHAPTER 17

During the following days, gloom settled over us all. When Patrick wasn't sleeping he was staring off into space, as if lost in his own little world. I wished more than anything that I could know what was going on inside his mind, but we were now back to him crawling deep inside himself and shutting off those around him.

I'd learned to just let him have his space and his quiet. His constant state of discomfort was hard on us all. That was the part I'd dreaded most: watching him suffer and fight a battle we all knew he wouldn't win.

And even though he was still here, we were already missing him.

He was discharged from the hospital a few days later, and though I wished for him to stay there so he could be in his doctor's care, he'd strongly pushed to go home. I was terrified knowing I'd see him struggle each night without being able to ease his pain. I wasn't sure I was strong enough to cope with what was to come.

I spent most of my nights alone in bed while he slept on

the couch. He seemed more comfortable there, or maybe he needed it to appear that way, but again I didn't argue. I had a strong suspicion that he felt as though placing distance between us would somehow shelter me from his struggles, but I saw them every time I looked into his eyes. I'd lie awake in the next room, straining to hear his breathing, seeking the comfort of knowing he was still here with me.

Today, watching Gage and Perry reposition the hospital bed Hospice had just delivered, I felt as if another part of my soul had been chipped away. Hospice's goal was to keep him comfortable, but they could only be here for a short time each day to offer support.

We'd reached the start of the downward spiral that we all knew was coming. I had never in my life been as scared as I was now. The things I'd read about that take place when a loved one begins to decline terrified me.

Closing my eyes, I placed my palms against my stomach, and our little girl greeted me by moving. It was almost as if she knew I needed that moment to remind me of my purpose —that even in all the darkness, there was a spark of light.

"Let's get you settled." I opened my eyes to find Gage had moved across the living room to the couch. Patrick looked up at him with that unhappy expression he had more often than not lately.

"I'll go when I'm ready," Pat grumbled as he looked past Gage toward the television as if he was actually watching whatever was playing on the screen. It'd been set on the same channel for days, but the volume was muted.

"Let me help you," Gage tried again.

"I don't want your help," he barked, and I flinched at the way his irritation rang throughout the quiet space.

Gage leaned in, bringing his face closer to Pat's and spoke very clearly, punctuating each word. "I don't give a shit if you want it, you're still getting it. It would make things a helluva lot easier for both of us if you'd stop trying to fight me and accept that."

I'd grown dependent on Gage over the last few weeks. I knew it was wrong, because he had a life outside this, but he'd been the only one who had the ability to handle Pat. Not once did he back down or get offended by Pat's outbursts, and I think Patrick knew he could speak freely to Gage. I also knew that deep down, buried beneath all that sadness and anger, was the Patrick we all knew would appreciate Gage's efforts.

I went to the kitchen in need of a break. When I sat at the table, the first thing I saw was the most recent sonogram picture of our daughter.

Thirty-three weeks today. That's how close we were. But I knew in my heart that the chances of Patrick being here the day Abigail came into this world were slim. It broke my heart to think of him passing without getting the chance to see her sweet face at least once.

Then I wondered if in his current state he would even want that. The thought immediately made me angry at myself. Of course he would want that. I don't care how pissed at the world he was.

"Sawyer." I jerked in surprise when Gage said my name. I took a deep breath and slowly turned in the chair to face him. "How're you holding up?" he asked as he knelt before me.

I nodded, though I knew there was really no point in lying to him. He knew me, so he knew this was killing me. I tried to look away when tears pooled in my eyes.

Then he was holding me tight. I buried my face in his neck and sobbed.

"Let it out," he urged, "just let it all go."

I wished then that Patrick was the one holding me close in his strong arms. I missed my husband's arms. I missed the way he'd always done everything he could to make me feel safe.

I SAT IN THE DARKNESS WITH MY LEGS CURLED UP in the chair, my body shielded by the large blanket wrapped around me. I'd thought of going to bed a long time ago, but instead I was listening to Pat's breathing patterns.

This was his third night sleeping in the hospital bed in the center of our living room, and though he hated it, I knew it was easier for him to sleep on than our old worn-out couch.

Each night after he'd fallen asleep, I tried to go to bed, but I eventually found myself back in the living room, watching him and listening to his breathing. I guess I needed it for my piece of mind. Though his breaths were weak and labored, I still needed to be able to hear them. I think in some weird way it was comforting.

When he was asleep he wasn't angry or pushing people away. He was just peaceful. I needed to see him this way, I guess, because the hard times were beginning to drown out those happy memories, and each day I found holding myself together more and more difficult.

The room was dark, save for the illumination from the light above the sink in the kitchen. The gentle hum of the refrigerator was the only other sound. I'm not sure at what point I allowed myself to fall asleep, but the sound of his voice jolted me awake.

"Sawyer."

I sat up straight and the cover slipped from my shoulders as I leaned forward, looking him over from head to toe. My heart raced as the thought of being here alone with him when something catastrophic happened. The moment my eyes reached his, I found him staring back at me.

"Is everything okay?" He shook his head, and my heart seized. I stood and walked toward his bed, my hands shaking as I did my best to stay in control of my fears. "What hurts?"

He lifted his hand and rested it over his heart.

I stared at him in confusion.

"I'm sorry." I could sense that whatever was on his mind was hard for him to face as his eyes shimmered with unshed tears. "Please don't hate me."

Suddenly it was hard to breathe.

"Why would I hate you?" I took his hand and offered a gentle squeeze. "I could never hate you, Patrick."

"I've been such an ass, and knowing this, but being unable to control it breaks me."

"You're going through so much," I said as I sat on the edge of his bed.

"So are you."

I closed my eyes for only a moment when he ran his fingers through my hair that hung loose over my shoulders. "I've allowed the fear to consume me and gave it the power to make me forget what I have. I'm just scared."

I opened my eyes, and his cheeks were wet from the tears he tried to control.

"I'm so scared how I'm gonna miss everything. I'm scared of not being here to protect you and Abigail." He took a shuddering breath. "I don't want you to be alone, Sawyer."

"I'm not," I said, cupping his cheek. Part of me knew he wasn't just referring to me not having any family at my side, but I refused to sit here and talk about the possibility of finding another man. It hurt too much.

"I know you don't want to hear this, but please just listen."

Panic raced through me, and I did my best to tame it. He needed this, so for him I'd listen.

"I need you to understand that it's okay." He took a deep breath. "I don't want you to ever feel guilty about moving on. A year, ten, it doesn't matter, because I know you love me. I know I'll always be a part of you."

I nodded. He smiled at me, and the sight of the tear that ran from the corner of his eye made my chest ache. "I want you to live, Sawyer. I want you to be happy. Promise me you will."

I couldn't do it. Agreeing meant I was agreeing to love again and I wasn't sure I could ever do that.

"I know what you're thinking," he added with a knowing grin. "Don't forget that I know you better than anyone."

"I can't promise you that I'll move on, but I promise I'll be happy for our little girl."

"Just so you know, Gage assured me he'd watch over my girls. So it helps knowing you'll have him here to protect you. Because if I can't be here to do it myself, there isn't another person I trust more."

I couldn't hold back any longer. I allowed my body to fall into his, and the moment his arms wrapped around me, I gave in to my emotions. I cried for all the things we'd miss out on and all the years we were being robbed of as my body shook against his.

"I love you," he whispered as his lips skimmed over my temple. "I'm sorry I haven't told you that as often as I should lately. But know that no matter how angry I get, or how sad and agitated, that my love for you never fades. I've woken up every day we've been together and felt as though I've fallen in love with you all over again. In the short time we've had, I've been given more than most have in a lifetime, and for that I feel lucky."

CHAPTER 18

"What exactly are we doing?" I asked as Luann and Willow led me to a table in the back of the church Willow attended. They'd shown up at my house bright and early to whisk me off for a day of pampering.

Now here I was three hours later with my hair and makeup done and wearing a new dress, but I still didn't know what the point of all this was.

That was until I stepped into the large room and found not only my foster mother Rachel, but every other woman Patrick and I knew. The men were still back at my house.

"Surprise," they shouted in unison, and I covered my mouth in surprise, though it couldn't hide my joy.

The room was decorated in pink and purple along with balloons that said *Girl* on them, and presents were piled on and around a table off to the left. Tons of food was spread out on two tables near the back.

"This is a party to celebrate my niece," Willow said with a huge smile. "It was Patrick's idea and we did the rest."

I closed my eyes and could almost picture the look Patrick

had had on his face when I entered the living room to find his mother and sister waiting for me. That alone should've told me he had a hand in this.

After crying with him for nearly an hour the other night, I saw what I could only refer to as relief in him. He still got angry and agitated at times, but the smile I had missed was back too. Throughout his discomfort and pain, he'd still found it important to do this for me, and for our daughter. That alone confirmed he was the greatest man I knew.

My day was filled with silly games, laughter, and presents. Pink everything would soon grace our home.

When the party ended and most of the guest had gone, I sat next to the woman who had shown me late in my life what a mother's love felt like. Rachel did her best with me, but by the time I reached her home, I was tainted with the idea that I was unlovable. That came from years of being tossed around from one home to another without being given a chance to find my place. But she didn't give up. Even when I'd hide away and ignore her efforts, she just kept pushing.

"Thank you," I said without looking over at her. If I had, I wouldn't be able to get the words I needed to say out. "I don't think I've ever told you that, and I should've. You took a rotten, scorned teenage girl who believed the world was filled with nothing but hate and sadness and showed her there was more to life than that."

"I knew there was love hidden inside you, Sawyer. I just had to help you find it."

We fell silent, I think because we were both lost in memories of me fighting her, and her continuing to love me even though I tried to convince her I didn't want it.

"You know I'm here for you, right?"

I nodded, still staring ahead as Willow and Luann loaded the smallest of the gifts on a cart—the bottles, lotions, and gift bags full of assorted items.

"No matter what it is, Sawyer, all you have to do is call." She placed her arm over my shoulders and hugged me closer. "Even if it's just to listen while you blame God and everyone else for the hand you've been dealt, I'm here always."

The knot I was oh so familiar with had formed in my throat once again. "Thank you," I whispered, trying to hide how raw I felt.

I looked up as a large man stepped behind Willow and found Gage standing there. He said something to Luann before he hugged her close. Then he looked my way and offered me a smile too, followed by a wink.

Gage had always been a part of our lives, the person who brought silliness and lightheartedness to every gathering and who could find the good in anything bad. But lately he'd become a rock for all of us. He offered to be the one we could all turn to when we needed to break, not just me but Luann, Miles, and even Willow.

He wasn't just our funny friend anymore. Now he felt like a soldier protecting people in the middle of a battle.

I also knew someday soon we would need to reverse roles and support him. The loss of the man he'd grown up with would hit him hard.

"THAT'S THE LAST ONE." I TURNED JUST AS GAGE set the last bag of gifts on the nursery floor.

He straightened up, placing his hands on each side of his waist as he looked around the room. "He wanted a nursery that looked like it came from one of those home-decorating magazines, and he got it."

The walls were pink from the floor to about waist height, and white the rest of the way up to the ceiling. A pink-flowered border broke up the two colors. A large arch led to the window seat that was large enough to hold at least four people. Pink, white, and yellow pillows filled the space, making it the perfect little cubbyhole for reading, naps, or really whatever I wanted it to be. The bedding for the crib was an assortment of beautiful purples, pinks, and yellows that pulled it all together.

"It is perfect," I agreed as I also scanned over the room. "Thank you for helping him make this a reality," I finally added as I refocused on Gage. "There was so much he wanted to get done, and I know without you here to help, he wouldn't have been able to make all that happen. That gave him peace, Gage—you gave him peace."

He nodded and his throat bobbed with his attempt to stay strong. "You plan on putting all of this together tonight?"

"As much as I can." I shrugged. "I wanna make sure he sees it finished."

With Gage I didn't have to express how important that need was. He already knew.

He knelt on the floor near the bags and placed each item into piles before him. When he looked up and saw me watching him, he arched a brow. "You gonna move, woman, or do I gotta do it all by myself?"

I laughed at his words, and it felt good. "Okay, Mr. Sassy." I tossed the wadded-up packaging I'd removed the baby monitors from at his shoulder.

"Oh, I see how you are." He shook his head and went back to removing the items. "Throwing things at the help," he mumbled, giving me a sideways glance. I could still see the smile on his face as I spun around and moved toward the dresser.

For the next couple of hours, we placed every item where we thought it fit best. It warmed my heart when I sat in the center of the finished room with my legs crossed before me as I looked around. But what made me weaken with an overwhelming love was when Gage stepped into the room supporting Pat with an arm around his waist.

Watching his eyes fill with emotion as he scanned the nursery was amazing. Then acceptance filled them, as if this was another thing he needed to see before he let go.

Offering me a wink, Pat gave Gage a weak nod, and Gage led him back to the living room, where he slowly drifted off to sleep.

CHAPTER 19

"All over now." Patrick's deep husky voice no longer sounded like him. It sounded like a weakened older man's, hoarse and barely above a whisper. "Still can't believe you gave her the house and everything in it."

"What the hell do I need it all for?" Gage said with humor. "It was all shit she picked out anyway, and you know I hated her taste."

I should have felt bad for eavesdropping, but hearing them cutting up reminded me of better times. I would miss watching them hassle one another, and I was sure Gage would miss it too.

"She did have shit taste," Patrick said, followed by a cough. "Look who she married."

"Hey," Gage gasped, placing his hand against his chest while gaping in mock offense, "what are you talking about, man? I'm a prize."

They chuckled.

"You are a good man, Gage," Patrick said after a few

seconds, "the best. I know I've asked a lot of you lately, but—"

Another pause followed and I leaned even closer to the doorway.

"I think it's getting close." I swear in that moment my heart stood still. "I can feel it, Gage, and I don't want to scare her, but I know it's coming. Everything is getting harder. Breathing, sleeping, all of it is nothing but a struggle. I've seen the fear in her eyes, that all-consuming panic. She doesn't sleep, she barely eats, and I know it's because of the stress this is all putting on her. She won't admit it's all too much, but it is."

"What do you need from me?"

"I need you to be here when I tell her I want to go back to the hospital, and I'll need you to comfort her, because I know I won't be able to." His voice was filled with sadness and disappointment. "I thought I wanted to be here when I died, but I can't do that to her. I don't want her to walk into our home and instantly be filled with that memory. I want her to remember me in all the good times, because this is our home."

Silence followed again, and as I rested my head against the doorframe, someone began sobbing.

"I just need a minute." It was Gage this time, and I felt his pain. "If you need me to be strong then, right now," he said hoarsely, "I just need a minute."

I wanted to go to them, but I understood this was a time they needed to share. In some way, I felt as if this was their acceptance of what would happen and maybe their goodbye. That idea broke me a little more.

"She's gonna need you to hold her up," Patrick whispered. "She'll fight you, we both already know that, but don't let her push you away, Gage. Please just take care of them for me after I'm gone." *Them* meaning our baby and me. I placed my hand against my stomach. "Protect them and make sure they have what they need."

"I will." Gage's voice was barely recognizable. "No one will ever hurt them." The conviction in it sent chills throughout my body.

"That helps," Patrick said, and I slid along the doorframe, lowering my body to the floor, feeling defeated.

"It's time," he said in his own defeated whisper and I had never in my life felt so empty. "I'm ready to say goodbye. I can't do it anymore."

I THINK WE'D ALL THOUGHT WE'D BE SAYING goodbye to Patrick in our home, surrounding him and holding him in any way we could. But it was his choice to return to the hospital. Part of me was grateful that the home we'd planned to raise our family in wouldn't be tainted by the memory of his death. Instead, I could remember all that was good, all that was happy.

Such fierce pain shot through me that it made me grip the chair arm and hold my breath. I couldn't hold back the yelp that fell from my lips as I let out a deep breath. Everyone rushed across the waiting area and knelt before me with concern etched on their faces.

We'd been at the hospital for close to twelve hours now, all on edge from Patrick's worsening condition. After Gage had regained his composure, he found me slumped on the kitchen floor sobbing and knew I'd heard everything they'd said.

After he helped me from the floor, he held me close as I tried to regain the strength I needed, only to fail. I rushed to the living room and spent the following ten minutes crying as I leaned over the side of Patrick's bed. Feeling his fingers comb through my hair as he did his best to soothe me even though he was weak and worn, only broke me further.

Now all the family gathered in the waiting area as the nurses settled Pat into a room. I'd thought I'd be okay now that the finality of it all had settled in my mind and I knew I couldn't do anything to prevent the inevitable. But with each passing minute, my mind raced with thoughts of everything I wished we would've done. All the things I should have said, those things I should have focused on. But no matter what, it never would have been enough time, because forever with Patrick still wouldn't have been good enough.

"Sawyer." Gage's voice pulled me from my thoughts. Taking in a slow, steady breath, I lifted my head to find him staring back at me. "Are you okay?" He was kneeling before me, his eyes widened with worry.

I took in one steady breath after another before finally responding. "Just had a sharp pain hit me," I explained as I leaned back in my chair, attempting to play it off as nothing. "I think I'm okay."

"Maybe we should have you checked out."

"Thanks, Dad," I said, expecting to get a smile or even a small chuckle in response. Hell, even an arched brow, but I got nothing. Just a firm, hard stare. "Okay." I caved quick when that same pain returned, only this time as I leaned forward, I felt a gush of something wet that frightened me. Instinctively I looked at my lap.

"What is it?"

I didn't even have to respond before he spoke. I guess he'd noticed the same thing I had.

"Get a doctor or a nurse," Gage barked, gaining my full attention along with that of every other person in the room. His eyes widened with worry as he leaned in close to me. "Fuck that," he mumbled, then lifted me into his arms and hurried through the waiting area toward the large doors at the opposite end.

"Gage, slow down," I tried to soothe, but he wasn't listening.

"I need a doctor," he announced, getting the attention of everyone in the hallway. I wanted to tell him he was being ridiculous, but then another pain shot through me. When I tensed in his arms and grabbed for my stomach, his panic went into overdrive. His grip on me tightened as he barked orders and demanded I be attended to now.

Soothing voices asked Gage what was wrong and I continued to focus on my breathing and my rising fear.

"Okay, sir, let me grab a wheelchair." I looked up to see a nurse hurrying away and returning just as quickly with a chair.

I could sense his hesitance, but after a few silent seconds, he slowly lowered me to the wheelchair and stepped to the side. But before they'd taken me far, he was jogging to catch up. "She's early," he said, still looking terrified.

"How early?"

They paused near the elevators and I looked up to see Gage's lost expression. "I'm just over thirty-six weeks."

Our nurse smiled and brushed my hair back from my face. "There's no need to panic, honey. I delivered my son at thirty-four weeks, and though he was tiny, he was mighty. Everything's gonna be just fine."

I didn't expect to be shipped off to the maternity ward still not knowing what had taken place with Patrick. I needed to be there.

"My husband's being admitted and I need to know what's going on with him." The nurse looked at Gage and then back at me with a puzzled expression. "This is my husband's best friend."

She nodded and the sound of the elevator's arrival echoed

through the hallway. "Let's get you upstairs and checked out. We need to make sure everything is good with you and your baby." She pushed me inside and tapped a button on the panel. "I promise we'll check on your husband's condition and keep you posted."

I wasn't completely happy with the fact I was now going to be four floors up from Patrick, but I had no choice. She was right; I had to think of our little girl too.

When we arrived on the maternity floor, I was thrown into a whirlwind of tests and questions. I could see the panic still in Gage's eyes, but I didn't have any time to make sure he understood what the doctor was saying. He looked a little lost; poor man had no idea what he was in for. So much was happening, and he continued to watch every move going on around him. It was sweet really that he was taking the promise he'd made to Patrick so literally. It was also almost comical to see him guarding the area as if he would run to my rescue if needed.

I was relieved when Dr. Haynes entered close to forty-five minutes later. "Hello, Sawyer," she greeted as she stepped closer and looked over at the machine to my left. "It would appear this little lady has decided she wants to come a bit early." Her gaze wandered to mine and the realization of what she'd just said hit me.

"I felt fine earlier," I assured her, worrying that maybe during the events of the last day, I may have missed some sign. "But then things got a little stressful." When her expression changed to one of concern, I continued. "They're admitting Patrick. We brought him in last night and I'm afraid he's not doing well."

"I'm so sorry to hear that, Sawyer." She wasn't just saying that to be kind. I knew she felt my pain. She'd been with me throughout the rough road after Patrick's diagnosis. She'd listened to me cry and talk about my fears more times than I can count. She'd also been there when Patrick showed such joy at finding out he was going to be the father of a little girl.

"Chronic stress, such as the situation you've been going through for some time, can cause long-term changes in your body. This is most likely what has led to your premature labor."

Guilt filled me as I thought of all the times I let myself grow overwhelmed with everything taking place around me. I should have been more cautious, more aware of the levels of stress I could and couldn't handle.

"Is she gonna be okay? "Gage finally spoke as he stepped up on the opposite side of the bed, placing his hand on my shoulder. "And the baby?"

When Dr. Haynes gave Gage a questioning look, I felt I'd better introduce them. "This is Gage, Patrick's best friend and mine." His features softened when I said he was my friend too. But it was true. Over the last few months, our bond had grown stronger and we'd gotten used to leaning on each other for support.

"It's nice to meet you. I've heard all about you from Pat and Sawyer during our many visits."

"You too," Gage said as he reached out to shake her hand.

"To answer your questions," Dr. Haynes went on, "yes, they'll both be fine. We are monitoring them closely. My only concern is you're not progressing, and with your water breaking and the passing of your mucus plug, we're now on our countdown."

Gage turned a little green at the mention of mucus and I couldn't help but smile I imagined him passing out or, worse, throwing up when things got a little more real. Poor guy hadn't signed up for any of this.

"What does that mean?" he finally asked when he regained his composure and his face returned to normal.

My doctor smiled at Gage because he'd continued to ask

the questions before I could think of asking them myself. "You're only a week away from being considered full-term. Generally at thirty-seven to forty weeks delivery is safe. I think if we gave you a little something to move along the delivery, it would be perfectly fine."

"But I'm not at thirty-seven weeks," I finally said. "Isn't that when you're considered full-term?"

"I have no concerns regarding the delivery of your baby, Sawyer. You've had no complications during your pregnancy and her heart rate is strong. Thirty-six weeks and one day isn't that far off from full-term. Everything will be okay." She placed her hand on my leg and gave it a gentle squeeze. "I think this is our best option at this point."

CHAPTER 20

P*atrick*

"AT THIS POINT ALL WE CAN OFFER IS TO KEEP YOU comfortable."

I stared at the doctor, hearing nothing I didn't expect to hear. I knew coming in that I would most likely be saying goodbye. I knew it was over—fuck, I could feel it. Everything was a struggle. Knowing that the hardest of times was near was the biggest reason I'd insisted on being brought here instead of continuing with Hospice.

"We've already begun the intravenous drugs to help with the pain." Dr. Sheppard stepped to the side to allow the young nurse to move in closer. The moment she lifted my hand to inspect the IV, I felt just how weak I truly was. I was like dead weight in her grasp.

"Your family is waiting to see you." I moved my head to the side, looking back at him again. My eyes drooped as I fought to keep them open. Exhaustion threatened to consume me as the room grew blurred and hazy.

"Sawyer," I whispered, though it took great effort to complete just that one word.

"Of course." He knew she was my rock. Though I loved my family and Gage with all my heart, she was who I needed at this point. That might be selfish of me, but I knew my time with her was almost over. I closed my eyes tightly as I tried to hold myself together. It felt like it was only yesterday when I stood at the altar watching her move toward me down the aisle. That long white dress hugged her body as she smiled back at me like I was her everything. I've said it before and I will say it until I take my last breath: she is my angel.

I jumped at the sound of Gage's voice. I'd given in to the effects of the medication and at some point had dozed off. I blinked a few times, bringing him into view as he stepped up to the side of my bed.

"How are you doing, brother?" he asked as his gaze roamed over the machines surrounding my bed.

"Sawyer?" I repeated my earlier request and a defeated look filled his eyes. Panic raced through me and just like that my exhaustion was gone. I might not have been able to get out of bed and demand to know what was going on, but I sure as hell could lie here and do so. "Where is she?" I sounded as if I'd contracted the worst possible case of laryngitis.

"She's upstairs." Gage placed his hand on my shoulder. "Her water broke a couple hours ago and they've admitted her." He paused and I let the meaning of his words settle in my mind. "Your daughter will be here within the next twenty-four hours, Patrick."

I closed my eyes and said a silent prayer for my wife and daughter. Though I wanted to go to her, hold her hand and assure her everything would be okay, I was too weak. "Go to her," I said, staring back at Gage. Telling my best friend to be by my wife's side while she gave birth to my daughter was so fucking hard. But it was my only option, and laying aside my jealousy toward him for being able to do something I couldn't, I trusted him with my girls. I knew he'd provide for them since I couldn't now.

"Tell her I love her," I said in a raspy whisper. "Tell her I'm with her, even though I can't be by her side." He nodded. "Take care of them."

I didn't just mean now, but forever. I had to know that no matter what the future held, they would both be safe.

"Go," I said and shrugged away from him. "I'll be right here wanting to see my sweet girl."

He nodded as he backed away with reluctance. I could only imagine the feelings that must be racing through his mind.

When he reached the doorway, he paused and his eyes bored into my own. "Hold on." His words were forceful. "Don't you fucking go anywhere, do you hear me?"

It was my turn to nod, and that movement would have to be enough to assure him I would do my very best.

CHAPTER 21

S awyer

"I'm gonna need one more hard push, Sawyer," Dr. Haynes coached. "Come on, you can do this."

Willow stood to my left, wiping the sweat from my forehead and whispering encouraging words. Gage stood to my right with tears in his eyes as he watched everything unfold.

When the contraction hit, I did just as the doctor had asked and gave it all I had left.

"There you go," she praised, "you're doing amazing."

I relaxed on the mattress as a loud, high-pitched, screeching cry echoed throughout the room. To me it was the most beautiful sound in the world.

We have a sweet little lady with a great set of lungs, I whispered in my mind, as if I could somehow let Patrick know that his daughter was here and we were both okay. I closed my eyes and a tear rolled down my cheek.

I looked to my left and watched as the nurse took Abigail to the table and began documenting all the things they had to for a new baby, like weight and length. Waiting to hold her was torture. I wanted to ensure she was okay. I wanted to count all her little fingers and toes and kiss her plump cheeks.

The moment the nurse turned to face me with my daughter wrapped securely in a soft pink blanket, my chest ached with a love that took my breath away.

"Here you go, Momma," she whispered as she lowered Abigail to my chest, and I wrapped her in my arms snuggly.

The tears pooling in my eyes were so thick that I could no longer see her adorable face. "She looks just like him." I attempted to swallow past the lump in my throat. "Just like her daddy."

I quickly lost the battle to hold myself together. Then Abigail and I were engulfed in a strong pair of arms, and Gage and I sobbed freely He offered me a strength I couldn't have on my own right now. I knew this was hard for him as well.

"I want to see him," I whispered and Gage pulled back just enough to look me directly in the eyes. "I need him to see her, even if it's only for a second. I need that, Gage."

He stared back at me for a moment before he looked at the doctor and the nurse. "We need to make that happen." It wasn't a request. "We need to do whatever it takes to get Sawyer and Abigail downstairs to Patrick."

Silence set in over the room as Gage looked at them, they looked at us, and then at one another.

"You know how important this is, Doc," he pushed. "These aren't normal circumstances. We all know that Patrick may not have a tomorrow. Hell, he may not even have tonight."

I could see how much the impact of his words had on

everyone in the room. Everyone paused for a moment as solemn expressions took over their faces. That glassy-eyed, slack-jawed look showed they were fighting to hold back their tears and remain calm. I recognized it so well. It was the same one that almost every member of our family now wore almost daily.

"Let me pull a few strings and see what we can make happen," the doctor said, and relief washed over me. "But in the meantime, we need to let them finish up with Abigail and with you."

"Okay." At this point I would have agreed to anything.

I HAD NEVER FELT THE COMBINATION OF EMOTIONS that I was currently feeling—a mixture of sadness, weakness, and love. I trailed behind the nurse who pushed baby Abigail toward Patrick's room, while she lay cozy inside the cart. Gage followed pushing my wheelchair as Willow walked beside us.

As we inched closer, the hollow feeling inside me grew. I had no idea what to expect, because no one would tell me his current condition. This to me meant that what I would find would be the one thing that would break me.

We paused just outside room 318, and my anxiety amplified as I took deep breaths. This was it.

Willow stepped forward and held the door as the nurse entered the room, followed by Gage and me. The first people I saw were Rachel and Luann, who stood near the foot of the bed. They lit up when they realized we'd brought the baby to see her father.

As we inched closer, I found Perry sitting at Patrick's side, lovingly holding his hand. "Patrick," he whispered, and everyone could hear it in the silence of the room, "there are two pretty girls here to see you."

My eyes filled with tears as they met Patrick's. He was exhausted, yet he found the strength to offer me his best attempt at a smile. "Hi, Angel." His voice was unrecognizable. "I've missed you."

"Missed you too," I confessed, unravelling more with each second. "I brought someone to meet her daddy."

His eyes widened a bit as he looked around the room. His movements were slow and his breathing labored as if that action took great effort. "Abigail?"

"Yes."

He closed his eyes, and his chest began to shake as he struggled to control the rush of emotions, only it was impossible.

I turned in my chair and looked back at Gage only to find that his expression was similarly heartbroken. "Can you get her?"

His eyes met mine, and his Adam's apple bobbed as he swallowed before he nodded. Willow moved me to the opposite side of Patrick's bed and I took his hand. He offered me a weak squeeze just before I pressed a gentle kiss against his fingers.

Perry moved out of the way so Gage could sit on the opposite side. I watched in complete awe as he gently laid Abigail upon Patrick's chest.

Silence settled again over everyone in the room as we watched in amazement. Patrick's tired eyes scanned over her again and again as if he couldn't believe what he was seeing.

And when he spoke I realized that what I was feeling before had nothing on what I was feeling now. I slowly began to break as I watched the man I adore speak to his daughter for the very first and possibly the last time.

"Hello, my sweet girl," Patrick whispered in a deep, raspy

attempt at words. But we all heard him, and slowly we all began to fall apart.

"You, Abigail, are why I've held on." I hung my head as my shoulders shook. "It was almost as if I could see you in my mind, yet that wasn't enough. I wanted to hold you and be able to tell you just how much I've loved you since the moment I knew you existed."

I lifted my head to see Patrick place the softest of kisses upon our daughter's forehead. "I told your mommy from the beginning that I'd get a little girl with her eyes."

I couldn't hold back my tears.

"Though I may not be here by your side to love you, Abigail, I promise to watch over you. I'll be your guardian angel, my beautiful girl, always." My eyes locked with his. "I'll always be with and your mommy."

That moment was Patrick's last coherent one. It was hard to watch him fade with each hour, but as a family, we all sat by his side and assured him that it was okay to go.

Though inside I was screaming, *No, please don't go. Please, just one more day. I need one more day*, I knew it was time to let him go. I needed to assure him that I'd love him always, but it was time he' found peace.

Through our sadness, somehow we were all able to find the strength we needed to say our last goodbyes. But that night, a part of me faded with him. That vibrant girl he loved fell apart and I didn't think she would ever return.

CHAPTER 22

G *age*

I'D PROMISED TO HOLD HER UP AND STAND BY HER side even when she tried to push me away. That was the dying wish of the best man I knew. Patrick had been a huge part of my life for as long as I could remember, and his absence cut me so fucking deep that I'd swear my heart was bleeding.

Yet I had to remain strong for Sawyer. She'd been through so much in such a short time. A moment that should have been a celebration had quickly changed to one of crippling sadness. I could see her withdrawing from everyone, slipping further and further into the darkness I knew she'd felt from the moment Patrick took his last breath, because that same darkness threatened me too.

She'd sat at the front of the funeral home, holding Abigail and staring ahead at the now-closed casket—the casket that held the man who'd taken a part of her with him when he said goodbye. From the place where I stood, I could see the deep longing in her eyes, a desperation for just one more moment with him.

That was also something I'd wished for. Holding it together was proving to be one of the hardest things I'd ever done.

"Has she talked to you?" Willow asked. I continued to stare ahead as she stepped up to my side and leaned against the same wall I rested upon. I shook my head. "I'm thinking maybe we should stay at her place tonight. I know she won't want us to, but I don't think we should give her a choice. She already told Mom she was going home tonight."

"I'd already planned to stay." Hell, even if I had to camp out on the front porch, I would be there with her. "She's gonna fight us."

"I don't care," Willow wasted no time replying. "Something tells me that you won't let that stop you, either."

"Nope," I responded just as quickly.

Silence settled over us as the pallbearers walked toward the casket. "I need to go," I said, stepping forward to join them. "Stay with her."

This was it, the final step before laying Patrick to rest. The day had been bad already. I'd seen Sawyer shed so many tears, I'd thought she wouldn't have any left, only they kept coming. I'd witnessed her sob with heartbreak until she could barely breathe. Each time she cried I swear it chiseled away another piece of my heart.

I stepped up to the mahogany casket and lay my palm against the coolness, doing my best to gain the strength I needed to get through this. I would never understand the reasons for cutting short the life of such an amazing man. He was loved, and he loved bigger than anyone I know. To take him just seemed wrong, especially when his wife and little girl needed him.

My tears threatened to spill, and fighting them seemed foolish. When I lifted my head and my eyes connected with Sawyer's, we just stared at one another. Her blue eyes almost glowed through her tears. I wanted to go to her and hold her tight. I wanted to tell her I was here for her, and that together we'd make it through this. Only I couldn't right now. But after Patrick was laid to rest, I'd tell her.

As we exited the church, Honor was standing just outside and I was surprised she'd even shown. Our divorce was final a little less than a week ago and we'd barely talked during the last month. When she offered me a kind smile, I felt like for a second that the girl I'd once loved had peeked through.

When we'd placed Patrick in the back of the hearse, I stepped aside and watched as the director of the funeral home closed the doors. An impulsive feeling shot through me, telling me I needed to open the doors once more and ensure he was secure, as if these men didn't do this type of thing almost daily. But this was Patrick. This was my best friend, my brother.

When I felt a hand delicately touch my shoulder, I spun to find Honor standing only a few feet behind me. She had that compassionate look in her eyes that I had so desperately needed to see so many times throughout the months of Patrick's decline.

"I'm so sorry, Gage." Tears filled her eyes, and part of me wanted to pull her close. Not so much because this version of her was want I'd longed for over the years, but because I needed comfort from anyone right now. Yet I refrained from doing so after thinking of how she'd been so dismissive of Patrick's illness and my need to be near him during it. She was selfish, and I couldn't forgive that.

"Thanks," I said just as I caught sight of movement over her left shoulder.

Willow and Luann led Sawyer from the doors, one on either side of her. Rachel followed closely behind carrying a baby bag.

"Excuse me," I said as I stepped around Honor, ignoring the questioning look in her eyes.

The women noticed me moving toward them, yet Sawyer kept her head down, clutching her daughter. I stepped in front of her and pulled her into a tight embrace. At first she hesitated, as if fighting against the comfort I wanted to give her, but her fight faded fast. She moved in closer, laying her head upon my chest and created a cocoon between us where Abigail remained sleeping soundly.

She began to shake and together we wept freely, not caring about anything around us besides our need to mourn a man we both would miss every single day of our lives.

"I got you, Sawyer," I whispered only inches from her ear. "I don't care what it is, what time of day or night, I got you."

She didn't argue. I think she knew she couldn't say anything to change my mind. It was more than just a promise I'd made. She'd become a part of me, too, more than she was prior to all of this. So protecting her was no longer about my commitment to Patrick, but about my commitment to her and Abigail.

They were my family, and nothing would ever change that.

⎯⎯⎯

I STEPPED INTO THE KITCHEN HOLDING ABIGAIL. She'd grown fussy, and not wanting to wake Sawyer, I snuck into her room and snatched her up before escaping quietly downstairs. Finding Willow at the stove already warming up a bottle for her, I focused on keeping her as quiet as I could.

When she found comfort in sucking on my knuckle as her little fingers curled around my finger, I smiled for what felt like the first time in days.

"I almost have it ready," Willow said, yet I couldn't look away from Abigail. She was so tiny, only weighing in at five pounds, ten ounces. Little grunts and groans, almost like those of a baby pig came from her, and my smile grew even wider.

"Here we go, Princess." I looked up as Willow stepped over to me and reached out for Abigail.

"I'll feed her." I didn't wait for her to agree before I took the bottle, then turned and walked to the living room.

The moment the nipple touched her lips, her head began shifting from side to side, and those little snorts grew louder. A deep chuckle fell from my lips as her little mouth wrapped around the bottle and she began sucking quickly.

"Hungry, huh?"

I looked away for only a second as Willow sat next to me on the arm of the chair and looked down at her niece. "It's amazing how much she looks like Patrick."

As I looked back at the sweet little girl in my arms, my chest tightened at the mention of Pat. Once again, I felt guilty for being granted this moment when he'd been robbed of it. He should be the one sitting here listening to each little breath she took and watching the way her cheeks moved with each suck on her bottle.

"You should've woken me up."

Willow and I turned toward the doorway to find Sawyer standing there looking frail and exhausted.

"Thought you could use the rest," I said and she gave me a displeased look. Sawyer didn't like anyone telling her what she needed. She never had. That was one of the things she and Patrick always butted heads over. But he just stood his ground with her. Honestly I think he secretly loved to ignite that fire in her.

Instead of coming back at me with arguments about why she was fine, she moved toward the kitchen and left us to tend to the baby. Dishes clinked against one another, and cabinet doors shut harder than I knew was necessary.

"Can you finish up with her?" I began to move Abigail away from my chest without waiting for Willow to respond. "I think I need to check on Sawyer."

Willow willingly took Abby and I walked to the kitchen. Pausing in the doorway, I watched Sawyer wash the pan Willow had used to warm the bottle, then place it in the dish drainer. She moved on to the coffee cup on the counter, which held the coffee I'd poured less than fifteen minutes prior.

"I wasn't done with that yet."

She jerked in surprise.

"I know right now it doesn't feel like it, but it will—"

"Don't you dare say it." It was my turn to be surprised by her words. She turned to face me, still holding the coffee cup. "It won't get better. Losing a part of yourself can never get better." Sawyer gripped it tighter. "It hurts, Gage, it physically hurts." She hurled the cup and it smashed against the wall only a few feet away from us. "It fucking hurts," she screamed as she sagged to the floor at my feet.

I hurried across the kitchen and knelt beside her.

"Nothing in my life has ever hurt this much." I didn't speak, giving her the chance to let go of her pain. "All those years I bounced around from home to home, never feeling as if I could be loved. All those times I got shipped off to the next place as if I wasn't worth the time, it hurt, but never this bad. No one has ever loved me the way he has, and now that he's gone...." She lifted her head, locking her baby-blue eyes with mine. "I feel so lost."

"Me too," I confessed. "I've always had him, you know. He was just a phone call away or a short drive." I paused, trying to control that deep ache in my chest. "I never meant we'd forget him, or that with time it wouldn't hurt. I think we both know it'll always hurt. When something happens and he's the one person we think of to share it with, it'll hurt because we can't. I just meant that with time it may grow a little easier to think of him without feeling as if we're being cut open all over again."

She nodded as if finally understanding.

"He was the guy I always turned to, and he was special, Sawyer. I feel raw, empty, and lost too. I just think we need to hold each other up. Just don't push me away, because I know you want to. It's how you work."

"Don't act like you know me so well." A small smile tugged at her lips and suddenly the air around us felt a little less thick.

"I know you, Sawyer." I took her hand. "Which means you also know me, and you know that even if you push me away, I'm still gonna be here."

I wouldn't let her fall.

CHAPTER 23

S awyer

It'd been a week since we'd buried Patrick. Each day I woke up telling myself that today I would celebrate his life, only to fall back into the darkness that consumed my every thought. It was ugly, hateful, and it made me into a person I didn't want to be, but I couldn't control it.

I wanted to know why he'd been taken from me, yet no one had the answer.

After I'd place Abigail back into her crib after her early morning feeding, I'd find myself on the back porch sitting on the swing and staring off into the yard. At times I'd swear I could still see him. There he'd be working along the fence line, or riding the lawn mower shirtless, and it only made my longing for him stronger.

Sometimes when I closed my eyes and sat alone in the silence of our room, I thought I could hear his voice or his sweet laughter. I wished over and over to hear his deep snoring again, knowing no amount of wishing would bring it back. But that still never stopped me.

Willow and Gage had practically moved in with me, and though I appreciated their efforts, I just wanted to be alone. I wanted to be able to mourn and fall apart without either of them freaking out and attempting to console me. I didn't want to be comforted. I wanted to hate God and everyone around me. I wanted to hide away and not be forced to smile when all I felt like doing was crying.

Then I'd think of Abby and know I couldn't.

I jolted in surprise at the squeak of the screen door and looked to my left. Gage emerged onto the porch carrying a blanket over his arm and a cup of coffee in each hand. The steam lifted from each cup as he walked toward me with a concerned expression that made my chest tighten with familiar anxiety.

"It's a little cold out here," he said as he handed me a cup. "I brought this too."

I didn't reply as he draped the blanket over my legs, then sat on the swing next to me. We sipped our coffee in silence.

Gage and Patrick had always been so close both in size and in the way they handled things. But while at one time Patrick was more hands-on while Gage was more standoffish, lately I'd seen another side to him. Part of me wanted to lean into him and allow my mind to believe for a moment that Pat was holding me close, yet I knew there were so many things wrong with that impulsive thought. Gage was not and could never be Patrick.

"I've seen you out here every morning," he finally said. "I've watched you smile and close your eyes as if some thought or memory has hit you."

Tears formed in my eyes as I looked away from him, trying my best to hide my reaction.

"Is that what you're doing? Remembering him?"

I nodded because I couldn't even form a simple word at the moment.

"I do that too, you know." I shifted on the porch swing and finally looked at him to find tears pooling in his eyes as well. "Sometimes when I'm sitting in the living room, watching a game or even some sports announcer recapping the highlights, I look over at that damn recliner expecting to see him there." He swallowed and let out a long, slow, calming breath. "Last night I had this dream that he'd called me." He finally looked over at me. "It was all so real. He was excited and out of breath, and you wanna know what he called to tell me?"

I wasn't sure I did. I had a feeling it would break me.

"He called to tell me that Abigail said her first word." A single tear ran along his cheek. "Daddy."

I stared at him, and with each passing second, I felt myself crumbling. Gage wasn't telling me these things to hurt me. He, too, was in need of someone to support him. I just wasn't sure I could be that person.

"I've been thinking," I said, trying my best to forget what he'd just told me. "You and Willow have been so good about helping out, but I know that you both have lives to get back to. You have work and she has the church."

"I took time off." I already knew this, but I also knew that time was dwindling.

"I know you promised Patrick, but Gage, that was unfair."

"And how's that?"

"Abigail and I aren't your responsibility," I said and immediately felt like an ass. "I just think that maybe I need to heal on my own."

"What you really mean to say is that you want to hide out and ignore everyone around you." He stared at me as if daring me to tell him different. "I may have made a promise to Patrick, but over time that promise became more, Sawyer. You and Abigail are my family. You were before and you are now. Family doesn't turn their back on family when they need one another." I started to speak, but he shook his head and stood from the swing, making the blanket draped over our laps fall away. "You can feed me all the shit you want about needing to be alone, but I think we both know that's nothing but lies. The only thing you want is to push everyone away. But I got news for you." He leaned in close, giving me that intense look of his, the one I'd only seen a time or two when he was worked up about something. "You can push all you want, Sawyer, but I'm not going anywhere."

Before I could speak, he turned and walked back toward the door and allowed it to slam a little too hard when he stepped inside, leaving me alone with my thoughts.

I stared off again into the empty space where my husband used to be. He loved working in the yard, even if it was something as simple as mowing the lawn. I knew then that I would never be able to look around this land and not picture him doing some menial task.

For the first time in longer than I could remember, I smiled.

"I'M THINKING A LIGHT GRAY, MAYBE." PATRICK TURNED FROM SIDE to side, looking over the old barn that sat less than one hundred feet from our back porch. The paint was flaking and some of the boards along the bottom had rotted and needed replacement. "Or we could go with that brick-red color and then paint the shutters on the house the same color."

I'd long ago given up the decision-making about the barn and simply watched him from the porch instead. It was much more pleasurable. He'd taken his T-shirt off and tucked it in the back pocket of his jeans, and his big work boots had dried mud along the soles from trudging around the damp soil in the yard. He was such a beautiful man, flawless in my eyes.

"Babe." I looked up from my perusal of the man who held my heart and found him staring back at me with a knowing smirk. "Red?"

My cheeks heated. I'd have thought I'd be able to control my blushing by now, but each day with Patrick felt like the first. "Red is perfect."

For a moment we simply stared at one another, him with that adorable crooked smile and me with what I was sure was the silliest grin. After an extended pause that made my heart race, he moved toward me. Each step made my adrenaline spike, and the moment his boots clunked against the wooden steps that led to me, I sat up a little straighter.

"You should know by now that when you look at me that way, it leads to very dirty things." He placed a hand on either side of me, caging me in my chair. "You get more beautiful every day," he whispered as he leaned in closer and brushed his lips over mine. "I still don't understand how I got so lucky to find you, but I thank God every day, baby. You're my heart."

With one swift and impressive move, he lifted me from the chair.

"Forget the barn." He skimmed the side of his nose over my own. "All I want to do is get lost in you."

I LIFTED MY HAND TO WIPE AWAY THE FRESH TEARS on my cheeks. Memories of Patrick still hurt so much, but I couldn't ignore them. I had to power through the pain; I needed to.

Gage was right. One day maybe that ache wouldn't be so crippling. Maybe someday I'd be able to think of him with happiness instead of pain.

Maybe one day.

I couldn't be afraid of the life that lay ahead. For Patrick, I couldn't be afraid.

CHAPTER 24

G *age*

"HOW ARE YOU HOLDING UP?" I LOOKED UP JUST AS Dalton, a friend and fellow firefighter, sat in the chair next to mine. I'd been watching a sitcom yet I didn't know a damn thing that had taken place.

"I'm good." It was what I said every time anyone asked. I didn't have time to break; I had to stay strong.

In the weeks since Patrick passed, things had grown a little less tense around the Cooper home. Sawyer still didn't like that I'd refused to go home yet, but I still thought staying was for the best. It was bad enough I'd gone back to work and couldn't be with Sawyer and Abby every night. Those nights were the hardest, but Willow filled in when I couldn't be there.

"You know that's what everyone says when they're anything but okay, right?"

I focused on the television, still missing everything that unfolded on the screen. It was like tunnel vision, but even then I couldn't tune him out. My leg began to bounce anxiously, almost on impulse, as I tried to hold my shit together.

"I'm good," I repeated. "I have to be."

I saw movement out of the corner of my eye and turned to him as he leaned over and placed his elbows on his knees, staring down at the floor in uneasiness. "I lost my brother when I was twelve. He was fifteen and he'd been my best friend since I think the day I was born. We did everything together." My chest tightened painfully. "He went with a friend to ride four-wheelers and there was an accident. They say his death was instant, but that day I felt like a part of me died with him. I know your situation is different, but we both still lost a brother. You and Pat were brothers, even though you weren't related."

"He was my brother," I agreed, "in every way that mattered."

"You've held your shit together, Gage, every day. I've watched how you've kept your feelings hidden for the sake of others. You've guarded Sawyer and Abigail, making sure they get everything they need, but you also need to remember that you need to grieve too."

"You don't think I know that?" That ache inside me grew again, almost to the point of controlling me. "I've grieved, Dalton, every fucking time I walk inside his house. Every time I see his wife and his daughter, I grieve for him."

"But you need to grieve for you." I squinted at him in confusion. "You need to let go of all that anger and hate before you explode. Believe me, I know, though a twelve-year-old may handle things differently than a twenty-eight-year-old man, but the point is the same: you need to break."

He was right, but Sawyer and Abigail came first, and for them I'd be strong.

Before I could get into it any further, the alarm sounded and our intense conversation was quickly forgotten.

"YOU, LITTLE ANGEL, ARE BRUTAL." I HELD MY breath as I moved the dirty diaper to the side of the changing table before sliding a clean one beneath Abby. I was becoming a seasoned pro at diaper-changing. A quick shake of the powder and then good as new. "Someone as tiny as you shouldn't smell so lethal."

I fastened the last strap of her diaper and heard a muffled giggle from the doorway. My eyes locked on Sawyer's and for a few silent seconds I took in her smile, which I hadn't seen much over the last month. However, with each day since our heated conversation on the back porch, she was coming around a little more. I'd still find her crying at times and I'd leave her to her tears. It was good for her to feel and not hide.

Yeah, call me a hypocrite.

"You think this is funny, do ya?"

"Oh yes." Sawyer's smile widened. "A full-grown man, all tough and indestructible, falls at the feet of an infant."

"An infant that shits like a full-grown man."

"That's nasty," she said, wrinkling her nose.

"Tell me about it." I tried to refrain from breathing through my nose. "I think she saves the best ones for the times she knows I'll be handling them. What do you feed this kid anyway?"

"Breast milk," she said, still smiling wide.

"Well, then that"—I pointed to the dirty diaper—"is all

your fault." I scooped up Abigail and snuggled her in close to my chest as I moved to the door. "So I'll take the cuteness and we'll leave you to handle the disposal of that offensive thing."

She narrowed her eyes and I chuckled as I moved from the room, smiling down at the cooing one-month-old angel in my arms.

Just as I reached the landing there was a loud knock on the door.

Perry and Luann had been coming over every Sunday to spend time with Abigail. The idea was to get Sawyer out of the house for a few hours, though for the last few attempts, she'd chosen to stay right here. But today that would change, even if it meant I would be carrying her ass to my Tahoe and tying her to the seat.

I opened the door and received a smile from two people who felt almost like a second set of parents. "Sure, you all waited until I changed the nastiest diaper in the history of diapers before you showed up."

Perry chuckled and pointed to Luann. "She does the diapers, Grandpa just does the cuddles."

I offered Abby to him because he was almost vibrating with the need to hold her. Seeing Perry practically fall apart at just the sight of Abigail made my chest ache. The way he watched her with his eyes shining with unshed tears told me he'd seen the same thing I did each time I looked at her.

Patrick.

She had his hair, his nose, the same shape of eyes; it was all there.

"She looks more like him each time I see her," he whispered, though I'm not sure he was speaking to anyone in particular. "That dimple," he added as he placed his fingertip against her cheek and slowly traced over the space he was referring to. "Even though he's not here in physical form, my boy is still here within her."

Fuck, that was like a punch to the gut.

"Yes, he is," Luann said as she leaned in and rested her head on Perry's shoulder. "He's still here with all of us."

CHAPTER 25

S *awyer*

"CAN'T WE JUST PICK IT UP AND HEAD BACK HOME to eat?" I trailed behind a persistent Gage, knowing arguing would get me nowhere, but trying nonetheless. "We could even grab something for Luann and Perry."

"They ate before they came over." He didn't even turn around to look at me. Stubborn man. I swear he only got more stubborn with each day. "And we'll be eating here." He finally turned to face me when he held open the door to the café. "So scoot, and find us a table, woman."

I stopped a few feet away and crossed my arms over my chest, arching a brow.

"You think that's gonna work?" He actually chuckled. "I know you don't want to create a scene and bring attention to yourself. I also know you aren't going to argue." He motioned toward the door and I fought a smile. He was so much like Patrick at times, it was scary.

"You are such a brat," I mumbled as I moved past him into the café.

His chuckle deepened. "A brat?"

"Yes," I said as I sat in the booth in the farthest corner. "It was much better than calling you an ass."

"True." Gage picked up the menu tucked behind the ketchup bottle and the napkin container. "So what are you in the mood for? Burgers?" He scanned over the items. "Please don't say salad."

"What is wrong with salad?"

"All Honor ever kept in the house were salads, fruits, and vegetables. I swear, I had to hide shit so she wouldn't throw it away." He finally looked back at me with the most serious expression. "I hate salad."

I couldn't stop the laughter that spilled from my lips. It felt good to laugh, and it was becoming easier each day.

"In that case, I think I'll order the biggest salad they have." I laughed again when he narrowed his eyes at me. When a waitress stepped up to our table, Gage just watched in silence and waited for me to order.

"I think I'll take a house salad with ranch." I giggled when he groaned, and the girl just looked at him in confusion. "You might want to bring him one, too, because he loves salad." His eyes widened just a fraction, though I didn't give him time to argue before I moved on. "I'll also take a bacon cheeseburger, no pink, with a side of chili-cheese fries and a Coke to drink."

"And for you, sir?"

"I'll have the same, only make my burger a double, with everything, and hold the salad."

For a split second the waitress looked confused, then she nodded and turned to walk back to the kitchen.

132 | C. A. HARMS

"You, Sawyer, are a bigger smart-ass than I ever gave you credit for."

I shrugged because there was no point in denying it. Before Patrick's death, I was always the one to keep things interesting. When I saw a moment where I could be silly, I went for it.

I tried my best to enjoy my lunch, though a part of me felt guilty for it. But I understood that Patrick wouldn't want me to feel that way.

Gage and I quickly got lost in conversation, and it was the first time in longer than I could remember that I didn't feel like the world was closing in around me. I was comfortable with Gage. The friendship we'd developed was the one thing keeping me above water. He refused to let me fall into that darkness that I knew lingered for both of us. I realized getting out of the house, if even only for a few hours, was in fact a good thing.

"Wow."

At the sound of a voice, we stopped midconversation and turned to the side of the booth to find Honor standing there in her pointy high heels, with her perfectly styled hair. Her long nails were bright red, matching her lipstick. But behind that beauty was a nasty, hateful woman.

"I'm surprised to see the two of you out together looking all cozy."

"Why?" Gage asked. "Because two close friends can't go out and have lunch together?"

"Just seems odd is all."

I arched my brow and stared back at Honor as if she'd lost her mind. Or maybe my expression could be better described as saying, *Who the fuck do you think you are?*

"What seems odd is that you even took the time to walk over and make your presence known." I wondered if I'd said those words out loud, and when they turned their heads to look at me, I knew I had.

Gage had a proud expression, and Honor, well, not so much.

With a *hmph* and a wrinkle of her nose, she pivoted and walked out of the café, shaking her ass a little too much in my opinion.

"Feisty too," Gage added with a laugh, then lifted his burger to his mouth and took a large bite.

"How in the hell did you ever put up with that woman for as long as you did?"

"Why do you think I was always at your house so much?" he mumbled around a mouthful of burger. "You and Pat kept me sane during all those years of torture."

I wanted to laugh, but his serious expression had me second-guessing that urge. He either wasn't kidding or he was really good at acting.

THE DRIVE HOME WAS PEACEFUL, AND THE SOUND of Gage singing along with the radio was soothing. His deep baritone mixed with that Southern twang made me feel like I'd been wrapped in a safety blanket.

I felt lucky to have him in my life. Although I'd fought him and pushed him to the point where I felt like I was going to explode, he still stood by me. He'd made me realize I wasn't alone in this. Together we were able to mourn Patrick's loss, and I knew without a doubt that Gage was the one person who wouldn't try to fix me, or make me feel as if I was being ridiculous when I hit the low moments. Instead, he was by my side, falling apart with me.

As we turned up the lane that led to the house Patrick and I had bought with a lifetime in mind, my sense of peace only grew. I then realized what Gage had said held truth. It would grow easier to think of the man I would always love without feeling as if my chest was being ripped open.

I smiled at the memory of when Patrick and I first drove up this driveway, pulling a large trailer that held what little furniture we had. It was our beginning, and even though he was no longer here by my side to share my days, I still felt as if he was in some way.

When we entered the house, my smile grew even wider when I heard Perry baby-talking with Abby. His deep gruff voice telling her about how sweet her "widdle button nose" was, was one of the cutest things I'd ever heard. I looked to my left to find Gage beaming too.

"That man is sunk," he said, trying to hold back his laughter. "She is gonna break a lot of hearts over the years. I hope you're prepared to handle the backlash."

"Nah," I murmured, "I'll just direct them to Uncle Gage. You can take care of it all."

For a split second a sense of ownership flashed in his eyes. "Damn right Uncle Gage will take care of it." He squared his shoulders and held his head higher. "That little girl and her momma will always have me here to fix whatever's wrong, and trying my hardest to fix even the things that may be impossible."

A few silent moments passed between us as we stared at one another, just before Luann's voice echoed down the hall, breaking the trance.

"I thought I heard the two of you come in. How was lunch?" She pulled me in for a big hug just as she has always did.

"It was good, thank you."

She looked over my face slowly and I felt a little uneasy until she spoke. "That smile of yours was always his weakness, and he was right." I tilted my head to the side, confused. "It does make everything seem as if it'll be okay."

My heart ached all over again, but this time it wasn't with crippling devastation but with happiness.

My time with Patrick was short, but it was powerful. Each time someone shared a memory about him or something he'd said about me or the love we shared, it gave me peace. Because I knew that even though I didn't get forever with him, our love was real and he knew how much I adored him. Patrick gave me so much in such a small window of time that I would always be thankful for what we were able to share. He'd been the one to show me that I was full of so much love that the world needed to see it. He gave me hope, and even after he was gone, he still found his way into the moments I needed him most.

"Thank you," I whispered to Luann, and her eyes shined with unshed tears as she nodded. She knew what I was thanking her for without even needing to ask.

CHAPTER 26

G *age*

I'D LOST TRACK OF JUST HOW LONG I'D BEEN sitting on the ground near Patrick's grave, listening to the leaves rustle. I came here often, more often than I shared with others. It was my time with Patrick; my chance to share my fears, or my dreams.

The guilt I'd been feeling for the time I'd been allowed to spend with Sawyer and Abigail had been lying especially heavy on me today because he should be the one here with them. It was the three-month anniversary of the day we said goodbye. The day he closed his eyes and faded slowly before us.

Fuck, I felt like I was being stabbed in the chest as I stared at his headstone.

Loving husband, father, son, and friend. Remembered by his family always.

I left the cemetery feeling no less sad as I drove back into town. I'd told Sawyer I'd be over later, only I couldn't seem to bring myself to go there. Last night I stood in the doorway of Abigail's bedroom and watched as Sawyer sat on the floor with Abby lying on a towel before her. Abby waved her tiny legs and arms as her coos and little grunts mixed with Sawyer's laughter. Gently she rubbed lotion over Abby's body before putting her in her pajamas and lifting her from the floor to hold her close to her chest. She pressed a soft kiss to her forehead and whispered, "I love you, sweet girl."

As I watched this beautiful moment, it pulled at my heart and something changed. Or maybe I should categorize it as having a revelation, because I realized I was feeling things for Sawyer that I had no right to feel. It terrified me and made me feel like a worthless friend.

I left, but instead of going to my apartment, I drove to the one place where I'd find two of the most supportive people I've ever known.

I smiled when I pulled into the driveway and saw my mother sitting on the front porch reading. A retired English teacher, she still held such a powerful love for books. She loved holding them so much that she'd thought I was insane when I offered to buy her a Kindle.

At the sound of my car door shutting, she looked up and her face lit up with that smile that still made me feel like a kid. "There's the most handsome man in Alabama come to see his momma."

"You should know by now that I can't stay away from my favorite place. Everything is always better here."

"Now you're just trying to make your mother feel good."

I reached the landing and moved to her, offering a big hug. "I mean it, Ma."

As I pulled back and took a seat on the chair opposite hers, she watched me carefully. I was sure she'd mapped out the trouble written all over my face. She'd always had a way of seeing right through me when I was feeling down.

"Tell me all about it," she insisted, "so then I can get to work on fixing whatever my boy is worrying over."

"I'm not sure if I want you to know the things going through my mind. It may change your opinion of the man you raised."

"Never," she said without hesitation. "You've always worn your heart on your sleeve, Gage. You've always held everyone up and taken care of those around you. You're a guardian, ready to do all he can to make things right. I know whatever it is that has you mixed up, it's nothing you intended to do."

"Even if I tell you that...." I paused because I still wasn't sure what I was feeling. My mother didn't speak, but waited for me to find the right words. "He trusted me to take care of them, to watch over them," I continued, hanging my head, feeling not just ashamed but afraid of what I'd see on her face if I looked up. "He never told me to fall for her."

"Is that what you've done?"

"I don't know, maybe." Panic rose in my chest. "I've been with them daily, watching over them. I've shared Sawyer's sadness and worries. I'm not sure if what I'm feeling is real or because of some screwed-up game of house. I just know I feel like I'm drowning. I feel like everything is closing in around me, and the worst part is, I feel like a jackass." Tears pricked my eyes. "I feel like I'm disgracing Patrick's memory."

"You aren't that kind of man, Gage." My mother slid forward and reached out to take my hand. "Before this, had you ever felt even an inkling of attraction toward Sawyer?"

"Never."

"Do you ever think Patrick had a reason for being so insistent that you be in his girls' lives?" With a gentle squeeze she forced me to look at her by leaning in closer. "You were the only person he trusted to be there for them. There was a reason for that."

"Yeah, he *trusted* me." Yet here I was, feeling shit I shouldn't be feeling.

"You were the only person he held that kind of faith in, Gage."

I'd held back my need to fall apart for so long, sharing memories with Sawyer or getting lost in my own thoughts when I'd picture Pat and me as kids. I was always able to remain strong and in control, and I'd never fully broke until now.

I hung my head as a sob escaped that I had no hope of stopping and my shoulders began to shake. My mother's arms were around me as she knelt before me.

"Let it go, son," she encouraged. "Break, Gage. Miss him, fall apart. I'm here to pick you up, I promise."

I couldn't stop the overwhelming grief that hit me.

He was gone.

The one man I'd always had by my side was gone, and I was left feeling so fucking lost that I'd begun to question if I would ever feel whole again.

CHAPTER 27

S*awyer*

"I THINK IT'S BEST I STAY AT MY PLACE FOR A NIGHT or two," Gage said as I held the phone tightly to my ear. "I'd hate to get you or Abby sick."

I nodded, why I'm not sure. He couldn't actually see me.

"Sawyer, are you there?"

"Yeah," I said a little too quick, then cleared my throat to cover up the fear even I heard in my voice. "Abigail's sleeping and I'm exhausted, so I'll be out the moment my head hits the pillow."

"I could call Willow—"

"No, really, I'm fine." But I was so far from fine. "Tomorrow we're spending the day at Rachel's, so it'll be good to get a good night's sleep. Honestly, Gage, we'll be okay."

I was met with silence and I could picture him pacing as he gripped the back of his neck.

"You're going to wear a path in your carpet straight through to the underlayment if you don't stop pacing."

His deep chuckle made my chest tighten with longing. I'd become so reliant on him that I was damn near having a panic attack at the thought of going without him. "There you go acting like you know me so well."

"And there you go pretending I don't."

Silence settled over us, the only sounds our mingled breathing.

"You'll call if you need anything?"

"Promise," I whispered as I closed my eyes tight. "We'll be all right. It's time I stand on my own two feet." Even if that thought terrified me. "You have a life outside of us. I don't think it's good that we both feel like we have to hold one another up every moment of every day."

"Sawyer, I—"

Part of me wanted to ask him what he wanted to say, but I let it go.

"Good night, Gage," I said with more confidence than I felt. "Take something and get some rest."

"I'll call tomorrow."

"We'll be okay."

I ended the call as I took in a deep breath. Looking around the quiet kitchen, I once again felt lost and unsure of what to do. I felt a heavy weight on my chest, like I was being swallowed up by grief and terror.

"I can do this," I assured myself with a shaky whisper before taking one deep calming breath after another. It was time I stopped relying on others and started relying on myself.

"I REMEMBER WHEN YOU FINALLY STOPPED thinking that one day we wouldn't want you here anymore." I stood in Rachel's kitchen as she rolled dough out on wax paper, moving the rolling pin left and right, back and forth until it was the perfect thickness. "You stood at my side, much like now, and asked me if I would teach you how to make my chicken and noodles. It was the first time you'd ever asked me to teach you anything, and I just knew you'd finally come to terms with the idea that this was your home. That we would always keep you here and safe."

The tears that had visited me at least once a day threatened to return. "You never gave up on that stubborn, damaged, and scared version of me."

"And I never will," she whispered. I knew she meant it. Rachel wasn't the type of woman to back down. She was loyal and her family meant everything to her, and Abby and I were her family. Harvey and Rachel could never have children, so for years they spent their lives giving lost children a place to call home, whether it was for a week, months, or years. I was the first and only one, though, who they adopted.

"How did you do it?" I asked, still watching her as she carefully and almost too precisely cut the noodles in a perfect width. "After all those years you had with Harvey, all the memories you made, how did you go on after he passed?"

"It wasn't easy, but I knew the life we shared was one that most dream of. We may not have been able to bear our own children, but we gave hope to a lot of kids who I think had lost it. We loved stronger and deeper than so many others we knew. We had a full life." She looked over at me. "The love you and Patrick shared reminded me of Harvey and me."

"I still struggle every day with even getting out of bed," I confessed as my vision clouded with tears. "Is that normal?"

"Normal? What exactly is that?" Rachel lowered the knife and completely turned to face me. "There is no timeline for grief. No certain length it should take for you to be ready to move forward. That, sweetheart, is different for each person, and don't you ever let anyone tell you otherwise."

Some days I felt like I could move on and live the life Patrick had wished for me. That maybe one day I could love again. Yet on other days, the idea terrified me. I didn't want to forget him, the way he smelled, or the way being in his arms felt. I'd never felt as safe and protected as I did when he held me close. I think the scariest part of all was not being able to close my eyes and feel that same security.

"Why don't you and Abby stay here tonight?" Rachel cut the noodles again. "I'd love to have you both here. We could finish these and then sit down for a game of Yahtzee after we get that sweet little lady to bed."

My tears quickly faded as I thought of all the times Patrick and I played Yahtzee with Rachel after Harvey died. I realized it had helped her heal. We offered her security even if only in small increments. I now knew what would help me too: surrounding myself with those I loved and learning to stand tall once again, even when that darkness hung over me. I'd get through this. I knew I would.

"Do you have ice cream?" I asked, and from where I stood, I could see her smile widen.

"Of course I do."

"Then it's settled. Abby and I are camping out."

CHAPTER 28

G *age*

"We're going for beers and wings," Eric hollered as we exited the station. "You coming?"

The idea of going anywhere but to see Sawyer troubled me. I should be on my way to her house. I should be making up for the fact I'd walked away without an explanation. I'd made a promise to watch over her and Abby, to care for them and keep them safe. Only I couldn't right now. Staying away for the time being was best. I needed to clear my head, because it was too fogged up. I felt like I was lost in the middle of nowhere with no hope of finding shelter.

"I'm in," I said as I readjusted my bag on my shoulder. "Baumhower's?"

"Yep," Eric yelled back over his shoulder as he walked to his old truck. "See ya there."

It was just after five and part of me wanted to grab my

phone and call Sawyer just to say hey. I'd spent the last three months with her, and though they weren't always full of laughs, we'd bonded in some crazy way. We'd built our friendship bigger and stronger. I'd only been gone for a little over a week, but fuck I missed her as if it had been forever. I missed Abigail too. That little girl could make everything better. But being with them had me feeling things I had no right to feel, believing shit that was untrue, and fantasizing about a life I wasn't meant to live.

It all disgusted me and made me feel ashamed.

Staying away was for the best, at least until I was able to get my head and my heart back to safe territory.

After a fifteen-minute drive filled with a whole lot of thinking, I pulled up to our favorite place for wings. I did my best to ignore the nagging feeling in my chest and that hollowness in my stomach that the girls' absence left. I talked and joked with the guys even though my heart really wasn't in it.

"Hey, isn't that Sawyer?"

I don't know who'd mentioned her name, but my head shot up and I looked around the restaurant. She was tucked back in a corner with a brunette sitting across from her, and I watched her though I knew I should've looked away. She was laughing and leaned forward, placing her hand next to her plate on the table as she had an animated conversation. I'd seen her do it so many times, I could almost hear her voice rising and falling as she carried on the way she did when she was into whatever she was' saying.

"She looks happy." I realized it was Ronnie who'd spoken.

"She does," I agreed.

Part of me hated the idea that she was having a good time without me, but another part was so damn proud of her for holding her head high. I wanted to go over and tell her I was sorry for disappearing, but with the emotions running through me, I knew I'd say shit I couldn't take back.

"Another round?" Eric asked the table, and I still couldn't pull my gaze away from her. The way her blond hair fell around her shoulders and the way her smile lit up the whole place.

When the waitress placed what I assumed was the check at the end of her table, my heart raced. Sawyer had been here within my reach all this time and I hadn't even noticed her. Now she was leaving and my time to watch her at a safe distance was at an end.

I felt like I was in in a trance as my gaze followed her every movement, my body completely aware of her presence. When she stood and grabbed for her purse, my stomach plummeted.

"Gage," Eric said, and I looked away for what felt like only a second. "Another?"

"No." I shook my head and looked back at Sawyer's table, which was now empty. "I'll be right back."

Before anyone could stop me, I walked to the open exit door. The evening air was cool against my adrenaline-warmed skin.

As I stepped outside, I looked around for her, my heart racing. I should've gone back inside, only I couldn't force myself to move. Then I saw her across the road talking to the same woman she'd just been sitting with. They were standing near Sawyer's car as she held her keys. She smiled again as the other girl spoke, then they shared a hug.

"I never thought you'd be that guy."

I jerked at the sound of a woman's voice just to my right. I spun around only to come face-to-face with Honor looking at me with narrowed eyes.

"You should feel ashamed of yourself," she sneered as her nose wrinkled in disgust.

"Oh yeah?" I shouldn't buy in to her drama, but my curiosity had gotten the best of me. "And why is that, Honor?" I shouldn't have grinned at her. It would only piss her off further, but I no longer gave a shit.

"She's a widow, Gage." My humor dissipated fast. "Your best friend's widow. Now here you are preying on her weaknesses, lingering in the shadows just waiting for her to fall so you can swoop in and be her hero. That's the lowest thing you've ever done."

"You have no idea what you're talking about," I snapped. I wanted to tell her that nothing I said, did, or even felt was any of her fucking business any longer. But she was hitting a nerve.

"Really?" Honor's eyebrows lifted in challenge. She crossed her arms over her chest and grinned, seeming pleased with herself. "Then tell me right now that you have absolutely no feelings for Sawyer, not even the slightest attraction, and I'll let the whole idea go."

A car door shut behind me and I fought the urge to look back. I could almost imagine Sawyer buckling her seat belt and placing her key in the ignition of her outdated Corolla. The desire to see her was so fucking strong, I could feel myself fighting against the pull of my body.

Honor smirked. "Exactly what I thought."

That desire turned to frustration as I stepped forward, crowding her. "What the hell do you want from me, Honor?" I asked, though I had no need to hear her answer. "All the years we were together, all those times I left for work, you didn't once give a shit that I was out there risking my life. Fuck, the only thing you ever cared about was your next hair appointment. Yet here you are in my business, acting like I give a fuck about what you think."

She had the audacity to look offended.

"Do me a favor, go back to being the selfish bitch you've

always been and forget I exist." I stepped around her. "It should be easy, considering that's what you became right after we said *I do*."

I yanked open the front door of Baumhower's and went back to join the guys, recanting my early rejection of another round. In fact, I had two.

CHAPTER 29

S*awyer*

ABIGAIL AND I SLEPT IN THIS MORNING AND IT FELT amazing. The sounds of her cooing in her crib through the monitor in my room made me smile. With each day I seemed to be doing that more and more. I'd started to realize just how blessed I was to receive the love I'd had from such a perfect man. He'd given me so much in such a short time.

Stretching my arms over my head, I giggled when Abby continued to coo and grunt.

As I went down the hall to her room, the light filtered into the hallway from the big window that overlooked the backyard. Each time I entered the nursery, I remembered when Gage carried Patrick upstairs to let him see it all put together. The pride in Patrick's eyes made this room even more special. He might not have completed it, but it came from his heart. He'd designed it, and with Gage's help it became a reality.

Each time I thought of Gage these days, I got that hollow feeling inside my chest that I immediately forced away. It'd been a couple weeks since he'd stopped coming over every day. In fact, he hadn't been here at all, though he did text often to check on us. I missed him being around. I admit I got use to his comfort, but I understood that he had his own life to live.

I paused in the doorway and watched Abby's wave her little arms and legs. She wasn't crying, only playing, and from the looks of it, enjoying herself immensely. I could honestly sit and watch her for hours just like this, being happy and so innocent. She gave me hope, gave me the strength to put one foot in front of the other and keep moving forward. She was my gift from Patrick that he'd left behind to remind me of the love we'd shared.

The doorbell rang, making me jump. I hurried across her bedroom and leaned over the side of the crib, reaching for her. Abby kicked her legs even more as I picked her up and kissed the top of her head.

"Good morning, Angel," I said as I hugged her close and breathed in her scent for just a moment.

As the doorbell rang again, I remembered why I'd hurried to pick her up in the first place.

When I reached the front door and looked through the sidelite, I saw Walter, our longtime postman. He stood with his back to the door as he looked out over the sprawling front yard toward his truck, which waited near the road.

As I inched open the door, he turned to face me and offered that same pitying look I got every time I saw anyone who knew about Pat.

"Good morning, Sawyer. How are you today?"

"I'm good," I assured him, and I was. Better with each, it seemed.

"Well, uh." He looked down at the large envelope in his hand. "I've got a certified letter here for ya."

I looked at the large envelope and the moment I saw the name on the top left corner, my stomach dropped to my feet.

Stratford and Whitton Pharmaceuticals, the company Patrick had worked for.

"I just need ya to sign right here." He held his tablet toward me and I took the little stylus that dangled at its side. My heart pounded against my ribs as my hand shook.

"You have a nice day, Sawyer," he said as he held out the package. "That sweet little girl sure does look like her daddy."

I nodded in agreement as I continued to stare down at the envelope in my hand. When the door was closed, I backed away and focused on taking one deep breath after another. I wasn't sure what this could be, as all our finances and even insurance policies had been settled shortly after Patrick had passed, or so I thought.

My husband had somehow managed to plan his funeral and pay for everything without me knowing. Part of me was angry that he'd done so, but I knew that anger had stemmed from the loss itself rather than from him attempting to once again shelter me from the pain that task would have caused.

He'd also managed to secure Abby and my financial future. I'd always left the handling of our bills and debts to Patrick, so when a check arrived for a life insurance policy I wasn't even aware he had, to say I was shocked would be an understatement. It was enough to pay off the house and live comfortably for a few years without worry.

Even though he was gone, he was still managing to protect me.

I carried Abby into the kitchen and placed the envelope

on the counter, then stepped back, just staring at it for a long minute. When she wiggled and fussed, I was able to pull my attention away and make her a long-overdue bottle.

As I sat giving Abby her formula, I found myself again staring at the envelope. Part of me knew whatever it held would most likely bring me to my knees, and that part wanted to avoid the contents. But I knew I couldn't ignore it forever.

Gage flashed into my mind and for an instant I felt the urge to call him, but it quickly passed. I could do this. It was just another step in the direction I needed to lead myself to stand tall and strong on my own two feet.

I avoided the large manila envelope for the morning, choosing to spend it happy with my daughter. We sat on the porch snuggled beneath a blanket as I rocked her and told her stories about her daddy. I knew she didn't understand, but that never stopped me from telling her. It was more for me, but she seemed to enjoy the sound of my voice nonetheless.

Even long after she'd fallen asleep, I continued to talk as if she was listening. I was stalling, I knew that, but I just needed a few more minutes.

When my arm started to ache from staying in the same position for so long, I stood and carried her toward the back door. As I stepped inside, my eyes immediately shifted toward the counter, and there, almost as if it was reaching out for me, sat the envelope.

I moved past it and took my time putting Abigail to bed before I returned to the counter. I took one deep breath after another, then reached out and without a second to change my mind, I tore open the edge and pulled out the contents.

With each word I read, my heart raced faster. My hands shook and tears began to fall heavily.

Please accept our deepest condolences on your loss of such a great man. His bright smile and kind heart will be forever missed. Enclosed you will find the check paid in full for Patrick's life insurance policy payable to you as his beneficiary.

Again, we are so very sorry for your loss.

I could barely see the words through my tears as I turned the page and saw a second page, which had a perforated section with a check attached at the bottom. The ground felt as if it shifted beneath my feet and my legs grew weak.

"Oh Patrick," I whispered hoarsely, clutching the letter to my chest as I leaned against the counter for support. I closed my eyes and tilted my head up as I again let the tears fall freely. "I miss you so much." That didn't even begin to describe how I felt.

I'd give anything to have him back, right here next to me. I'd give up everything I owned to share just one more day in his arms. Seeing his smile or sharing his laugh would be worth it.

Even though he was no longer here to protect me, he'd still made sure I'd have protection in his absence.

CHAPTER 30

G *age*

"WHAT DO YOU MEAN YOU'RE LEAVING?" MY mother was by far one of the kindest, gentlest women in the whole state of Alabama. That was until someone did or told her something she didn't quite agree with. Then they'd need to prepare for the fire hidden inside her.

"I'm going to Arizona, just for—"

"The hell you are." She uncrossed her arms and took a step toward me. "You're keeping your ass right here in this fine city of Tuscaloosa. Don't think you're too old and big for me to beat."

I chuckled as I hooked my arms around her shoulders, pulling her in close.

"I volunteered, Ma." She fought against me to loosen my grip. "It's only for a month."

"A month too long."

She was as stubborn as I was.

"I need to get away, for just a little bit and clear my head." I'd tried, but my feelings for Sawyer had only grown stronger. Hell, everywhere I looked, I saw or heard something that made me think of her. Which only led to me feeling like the scumbag Honor accused me of being.

"I've already cleared it through the captain and I've got enough time saved up to take off." Her body sagged as she gave up the fight. "I need this, Ma."

"What you need is to stop acting like those feelings you have are wrong." My body tensed, though I tried to act as though her insinuation didn't affect me. "You aren't a guy who targets helpless women. You can run away, you can try to ignore what you're feeling, but damn it, Gage, you can't just make it disappear."

"Mom."

"You go," she said as she pushed against me, and this time I allowed it. Looking up at me, she offered a smile, though I knew it didn't reflect her true feelings. "Clear your head and come back here, to Alabama, with a clear conscience." She lifted up onto her tiptoes and pressed a kiss to my cheek. "But know this"—her eyes again locked with mine—"if you come back still battling this nonsense, I will knock it right out of you."

I could have gone into all the things I was feeling, denying what she'd said, but what was the point? Honestly, this woman knew me better than anyone else.

"I will," I assured her as I hugged her close and hoped I could do as she insisted.

"Before you go, you need to pay a visit to that girl." My mother moved away from me and lifted the pot of coffee only a few feet away to freshen her cup. "I didn't raise you to be a coward and I know that leaving without saying a word to her is the easy way out."

I nodded as my nervousness grew.

———————

I LIFTED MY HAND THREE DAMN TIMES TO KNOCK, yet each time I stopped.

There I stood on Sawyer's front porch, a place I'd been to more than a hundred times, yet I couldn't bring myself to knock.

I spun at the sound of tires crunching against the gravel just as Perry's truck slowed to a stop next to mine. He climbed out and approached with a solemn expression.

"Hey, son." His greeting made me feel guilty all over again. I knew he'd feel different about calling me that had he known the things rolling around in my mind. "Willow call you too?" Perry stopped a couple of feet in front of me and looked toward the front door. "How's she doing?"

"Willow?"

He offered me a lift of his brow as he pointed toward the door. "No, Sawyer."

"I haven't been inside yet. I actually just got here." Okay, that was a lie. I'd been standing on this damn porch for five minutes or more. "Wait. Why did Willow call me?"

The front door opened and there stood Sawyer. Her eyes were red and swollen, and though it was two in the afternoon, she was wearing pajamas. She didn't even seem to register I was there as she moved into Perry's arms.

"I don't think I can do this." Her words were muffled, yet I could hear her clearly. "Every time I think I'm okay, like maybe today will be a better one, something happens and I'm right back to that same dark place."

"You can do this," Perry assured her as his eyes locked on mine over Sawyer's shoulder. "You're not alone, Sawyer, never alone."

I didn't think he was actually directing those words toward me, referring to my absence, but my conscience took the hit. The sound of Abigail crying had my feet moving before my mind could stop them, and I took the stairs two at a time until I reached the top landing.

I found her in her crib, her little fists rubbing at her tired eyes.

"She hasn't slept. She's crying all the time and I don't know what to do to soothe her," Sawyer said behind me, walking closer. "It's almost like she knows I can't do it too."

Abby lay her head on my shoulder when I picked her up, and her tears and slobber soaked through my T-shirt. "It's okay, baby," I whispered near her ear as I rocked from side to side. "Sh," I soothed as I rubbed my hand over her back. "Everything's okay, sweet girl."

Her crying faded, yet she continued to sniffle, and when she did, her little body shook. I smiled when she nuzzled her head against the crook of my neck and her tiny hand fisted my collar.

"I got you," I assured her, continuing to rock her while holding her close. "I'm not going anywhere."

Silence set in and I peered back over my shoulder to find Perry and Sawyer in the doorway. Perry smiled in awe as he looked at his granddaughter in my arms, and Sawyer stared directly into my eyes, as if she wanted to say something but chose to remain silent. That look made my heart ache.

"Let's go wait downstairs." Perry tried to move Sawyer from the doorway, but she shook her head. "You need your rest too. Gage has Abby."

"Until when, the next time he decides to disappear without so much as a phone call?" The hurt in her eyes gutted me. "You're right," she said quickly, like she was trying to erase what she'd just said. "I do need to sleep."

She turned and left as Perry and I stared after her.

I didn't want to let go of Abigail, because she was like a tiny human buffer between me and a serious-looking grandpa who was now eyeing me with curiosity. The longer we stood there, the more I realized I'd have to somehow get myself out of this mess. Perry and Luann were like family. I'd grown up between their house and mine, and the last thing I want was to disappoint either of them.

"You wanna explain what that was about?"

I turned my back to him and eased Abigail into her crib, then placed her blanket securely around her. I stood tall and pressed my palm to her stomach, focusing on the rise and fall of each breath she took. It calmed my racing heart.

"I'm sorry," I whispered without turning to face him. I couldn't look into his eyes when I confessed my wrongs. "I never meant to feel this way."

"What are you talking about?" Perry seemed closer this time, though he still whispered.

"I was just supposed to watch over them, make sure they had everything they needed. He told me to protect them, but he didn't tell me to...." I couldn't get the words to form. Hell, my chest felt so unbelievably tight, I'd swear I was on the verge of a panic attack.

Perry placed his hand on my shoulder and gave it a firm squeeze. "I don't know what's going on, Gage, but you need to talk to me, son." There that word was again, and before all this, before the loss of Patrick, I'd have felt blessed to have him refer to me that way. But now it only made my pain grow.

"I'm sorry," I said as I turned to face him, avoiding eye contact. "I can't do this."

I left the room and again took the stairs two and a time. When I reached the front door, I paused for only a second as I thought of what Sawyer had said.

"*Until when, the next time he decides to disappear without so much as a phone call?*"

She didn't deserve this, which was why I'd made the choice to free her from me. My ex-wife was right, I should feel ashamed.

Nine months later

CHAPTER 31

S awyer

"WERE YOU ABLE TO STOP AND PICK UP THE balloons?" I nestled the phone between my cheek and shoulder as I spread the pink icing over the final six cupcakes.

"Yes," Willow said with a laugh. "And the tablecloths and the streamers, plus the ice cream and the—"

"I get it." It was my turn to laugh. "I'm being a nag."

"No, you're just being a mommy who wants her daughter's first birthday to be perfect."

That's exactly what I wanted.

The last year hadn't been easy. I'd had a lot of ups and downs, and dark times had outweighed the bright ones. But I owed almost all of those bright moments to my sweet girl. If not for her holding me up over the last twelve months, I'd be completely lost.

Then there was Willow, who I'd grown quite close to, and Emma, my best friend from high school who I'd recently reconnected with. She'd tried a few times to get me out after Patrick's death, lunch here and dinner here, but I had to come around in my own time.

It helped that I had so many people who refused to let me fall. They stood by me through the good and the bad, and though I tried to resist their help, they gave it anyway. Now two days a week I'd go to church with Willow and we'd share our grief with others who'd lost someone they loved, either with or without warning. Because even when someone knows it's coming, it's still the hardest thing to face. No one can ever be truly prepared for a world where their loved ones no longer physically existed.

Yet throughout all the ups and downs, I still felt like something was missing—or more like someone.

"I'll be there in fifteen minutes to help set up," Willow assured me before saying a quick goodbye and ending the call, leaving me alone with my thoughts.

Gage had volunteered to go to Arizona nine months ago to help rebuild a church an arsonist had burned to the ground. It just showed he was the kind of man who always looked for ways to help those in need. He was meant to be there for only a month, but he had yet to return.

Something had changed in him, and one day he just stopped being that shoulder I could cry on. I blamed myself for his distance because it wasn't fair that Patrick had put pressure on him to take care of Abigail and me, and it wasn't fair that I took his help so easily. In the end, all I'd managed to do was lose another man who'd meant so very much to me. A man I trusted as much as Patrick.

I missed him. I missed the way he made me laugh even when I'd felt there was nothing to truly be happy about. I even missed the way he'd challenged and irritated me when he tried to tell me what he thought was best for me. I missed arguing with him too. I know that sounds unbelievably ridiculous, but I did. I'd wished so many times that I could go back and repair the distance that had developed between us.

"Where is our sweet little grandbaby?" Luann singsonged as she rushed through the front door. That was followed by the cutest little giggle just before Abigail barreled into the kitchen and her diapered bottom collided with the floor.

She'd started walking only a week ago and was still unsteady. On most occasions her upper body got ahead of her feet and she'd fall to her knees. That of course only led to her crawling the rest of the distance she wanted to go faster than the speed of light. She'd grown into such a happy girl, fun and full of so much energy it made my head spin at times, but I loved every minute of it.

"You think you can escape Grandpa?" I turned around just in time to see Perry snatch her up as her little legs moved a mile a minute. His face moved in toward her belly and the room filled with the sounds of him blowing raspberries against it and her giggling.

"Something smells amazing in here." Luann slipped up to my side and leaned closer to give me a one-armed hug. "What can I help you with?"

"Barbecue is ready. Just need to move it all to the dining room, and Willow should be here anytime with the table-cloths and the rest of the decorations."

Everything moved quickly after that. I had Patrick's parents and sister racing around, and Rachel organizing the food table while she snuck Abigail treats when she thought I wasn't looking. Normally the idea of her being hyped up on sugar would terrify me, but I figured with no nap and a whole lot of party activities, it all may even itself out. If not, then I'd gladly stay up late and together we'd further exhaust ourselves.

With each knock on the door or ring of the bell, I greeted those who came to share this day with Abby. They included people I'd met in the grief group as well as those I'd known since Patrick and I were married, and I felt blessed to have them here.

I won't lie, though. Each time the door opened, I'd hold my breath wishing for one specific person to be on the other side. As the party wrapped up and the guests said their good-byes, I felt a pang of sadness that he hadn't come.

I'd grown so occupied with my thoughts that I squealed when a splash of something cold soaked the front of my shirt and jeans.

"Oh damn." Luann knelt beside me. "I had the hardest time tightening that lid and I thought I had it on right."

There I sat covered in apple juice in the center of the dining room floor as my little girl looked up at me with the biggest smile, and all I could do was laugh. "Is that funny?" I asked her as I held my shirt out from my now-soaked chest.

Abby bounced up and down as if she'd just done something great.

"I've got her. You go change," Luann insisted.

I hurried to my room, and as I entered, I looked around at it, unable to hold back my smile. With my newfound acceptance of what my life was now, I hadn't just found a way to move forward, but a way to soothe my pain. My room now resembled something from a home magazine.

Redecorating was my new hobby. I'd found I had a knack for making something a little outdated and tarnished look beautiful again, so I'd redone the older, darker version of this room in bright colors. It wasn't easy to give away Patrick's things and donate his clothes to the church, but I knew he'd want them to go to someone who could use them. But Abby deserved to have a piece of her father, so I'd kept a couple boxes of his things. They were things I'm sure most would've just thrown away, but to me they were special. They included a note about something he'd jotted down to jog his memory later, written with that little swoop he used on the letter *S* and the strangest little curve he'd add when writing a *W*. I also kept the glasses he'd worn late in the evening after removing his contact lenses for the day.

I quickly grabbed for a shirt in the closet and hopped on one leg through the room as I pulled off my wet jeans. Forgoing my usual method of pulling up a stepstool to reach the top shelf of the closet, I jumped up and down, doing my best to grab the jeans I had folded and placed there earlier.

With one quick yank they tumbled down on me, along with a small box containing a handful of items I'd planned on going through when I had some time. They were things I'd found scattered throughout the room when I was redecorating, like papers from Patrick's side of the dressers or his nightstand. I hadn't really looked too close at them yet, thinking they were most likely old bank statements or bill stubs. Though they, too, contained meaningless scribbles to himself, the fact they were written in his hand made them feel like a weird little part of him I couldn't give up yet. As the items spilled from the box and fell to the floor, I looked down, and one specific piece stuck out above all the others—a legal-sized envelope with writing on the front that caught my eye.

To my beautiful Angel

I'm not sure how I'd missed the envelope before. With shaky hands I flipped the envelope over and loosened the seal, then lowered myself to the bed and unfolded it, my heart racing with the idea of what it held.

YOU ARE THE ONE WOMAN WHO HAS HELD MY HEART FROM THE *moment I first saw her. There was no hope for me, no way I could deny* the impact you had just from seeing you. You are gorgeous inside and out, and you are my heart and my everything.

I've spent the last few months watching you grow with our child. The times when you thought no one was looking when you'd place your hands over your small stomach and close your eyes for a moment, and your lips would move like you were saying the smallest of prayers. Each gesture only made me fall in love with you all over again. You've always been beautiful to me, Sawyer. I've been mesmerized by the beauty those moments held.

I know there will be so many things I'll miss leaving this world, but knowing you'll have our child to comfort you helps. Knowing you two will have each other is like a weight lifted off my shoulders.

You're an amazing woman, Sawyer. One built of strength and compassion. I know the future holds times where you'll feel as if you can't go on, but somehow through it all you'll thrive. You'll hold your head high and be the mother you were born to be.

That emptiness inside you will heal, and one day I hope you'll find the strength inside to live on without sadness or guilt. I know you don't like to talk about it, but please know that I want you to find love again. The love you've shown me over the years is too powerful, too perfect to hide.

Don't be afraid to fall in love again, baby, please.

I only ask that you do one thing for me. Don't settle. You deserve the world, my angel, and I want you to find a man that sees this too. Because if he can't love you the way I've loved you all these years, then, sweet girl, you aren't living the life you deserve.

You falling in love again in no way means you've forgotten me. I know you love me and that you always will. Our love was so great that what we've shared will never be forgotten. Just be happy, Sawyer, and live. You and Abigail deserve love and I want you to find that great love again. Be free and celebrate me. Don't mourn me. And know that I'll be forever by your side watching over you and Abigail. For you will both forever be my girls.

WITH LOVE ALWAYS,

PATRICK

I COULDN'T BREATHE. TEARS STREAMED ALONG MY cheeks and dripped from my jaw, and I did nothing to stop them.

He was right. With time, I had found the strength to move forward, to live on. The idea of loving someone again didn't terrify me as much as it had before. But reading his words and knowing he wrote them while he was probably only a few feet away from me both broke my heart and gave me strength.

I don't know how long I sat on my bed, holding Pat's letter. I wasn't even thinking about the people outside my room who were celebrating the life of the little girl Patrick and I created. I just needed this time.

CHAPTER 32

G *age*

"Well, look who's back." Eric stood from the chair in the small kitchen at the station and moved toward me. "Just to visit or are you back for good this time?" He leaned in and gave me a one-armed hug, slapping my shoulder.

"I was thinking I'd stick around," I offered with a chuckle. "I think if I'd decided to stay gone any longer, my mother would have killed me."

"Does the captain know?"

"He knows and he's still deciding if he's got a space available for the man who left him for a long-ass extended vacation." Captain Royce's voice echoed through the kitchen of the station.

I tossed a grin in his direction and found him struggling to hold back his own. "Vacations consist of long nights filled with drinks and relaxation, not days of sweat and exhaustion."

I'd intended to only be gone a month, that was true. But call me a sucker, I couldn't walk away until the church was finished. After I'd called my father, he agreed to move what little I owned out of my small-ass apartment and into storage, then he spent a week on the couch when my mother found out. Poor guy paid the price for my choice, but he had big shoulders and took it like a man.

I was proud of the work I'd done. Not only was the church I helped rebuild a place of worship, it also offered shelter for those in need. It even served as a daycare, and a place the homeless could come for a good meal once a week. People felt safe there, and during my time there, so did I. The work helped me clear my head a bit, and I was finally able to accept my feelings and understand that what my mother had said was true. I couldn't run from them; I needed to face them.

"I still have your place here, Gage," the captain finally said. "I told you I would."

He and I had also shared a heart-to-heart one night after I'd sat in my motel room putting away one too many beers. I confessed my feelings for a certain blonde and fully expected him to tell me how wrong that was, only he didn't.

"Some people will always think it's wrong, or that you planned to slip in and take Pat's place all along. But you know differently, and at the end of the day, the only two who matter are you and her. The others will either be forced to accept it or stay the hell away. It's that easy. If you live your life strictly by what those around you think, then you're a damn fool, boy, because you can never please everyone. The world is full of heartless, judgmental, and ungrateful people. Live your life, Gage, and stop worrying so much about the things you can't change. And stop running. You aren't a coward."

He was a good man.

"I expect you back here for the next shift," he said firmly, trying to fall back into the role of an authority figure. "Or that position I've held for you will no longer be available."

I caught the grin he was trying to hide as he turned and walked back to his office.

"Oh, and that apartment I was telling you about will be ready by the end of the week," he hollered just before he shut his door. Thank God, because though I love my mother, the idea of living under the same roof for too long was already giving me anxiety.

"I WAS WONDERING HOW LONG YOU'D BE IN TOWN before you came over and said hi." Perry leaned back in his recliner and lifted his beer to his lips. As he eyed me over the bottle, I felt like an adolescent again. I remembered all those times he'd lectured Patrick and me when he caught us doing crazy shit. He'd tried to be a hard-ass, but at heart he was one of the boys. Next to my own father, he was the most understanding man I'd ever met.

"Sorry, I, uh, got busy and meant to stop by, but...." The excuses rolling around in my mind weren't the truth. I'd been avoiding the Coopers since returning because facing them was hard. Their son, and my best friend, was gone, and here I was having feelings about the girl they'd watched marry their son.

"But you've still got some crazy idea that makes you feel like you can't face me."

I looked him straight in the eyes, feeling a little taken aback by his words.

"What?" he said finally, leaning forward as he lowered the footrest, then stood. "You still think after all these years that I don't know you well enough to figure out what you're thinking? It also helps that your mother and my wife can't keep their conversations down. I've heard all about these unsettled thoughts in your head for the last few months."

I swear my mother gossiped more than anyone else I knew.

"Boy, you've had your mother a mess. Had I not known about the good work you were doing in Arizona, I would have been on the first flight out there to drag your ass back here myself."

I averted my stare and focused on the space between us at my feet.

"So what is it, you think you've somehow betrayed him? Like you'd planned it all from the beginning?"

I shook my head, still unable to look at him. "I never meant for it to happen."

I looked up at Perry and saw he'd moved closer. "No one in their right mind would pin something like that on you. No one could have truly known this would happen." He walked toward his desk in the corner and opened the top drawer before turning back to face me. "But I think somehow he did."

"What?" My mind raced at the idea that Pat could have thought of me as a threat. That he'd passed thinking I'd felt something for his wife all along. My stomach plummeted and nausea hit me hard.

Perry paused only a few feet away from me as he looked down at the envelope in his hands. "Patrick gave me two letters and asked me to hold on to them until I felt the time was right." His lips pursed and his nostrils flared as if he were fighting off emotions he desperately wanted to hide. "One was addressed to the man who has chosen to love Sawyer. That one is a lot shorter than the other and is pretty much a warning."

The idea of someone touching Sawyer or holding her infuriated me, and I knew I had no right to have those feelings.

"And the other was addressed to you, the man he trusted with his girls." He turned the envelope to face me, and that was exactly the way it was written on the front in penmanship I recognized. *To the man I trust more than any other. My best friend, Gage.*

"Like I said, I think he knew"—Perry held out the envelope—"or at least he hoped things would play out a certain way.."

"I don't understand." My voice was a hoarse whisper and the pain of grief in my chest rose to my throat.

He pushed the letter a little closer. "Read this, and then you will."

When I took the letter, he turned and walked from the room, leaving me alone in the house Patrick grew up in.

I needed a few minutes to gain the strength to read it, but as I did, my eyes filled with tears.

IF WHAT I FEEL IN MY HEART IS TRUE, I ALREADY KNOW WHO'LL BE the one to hold dear the two most precious people to me. There's no one I trust more, Gage. There is no one I believe to be able of loving my family the way I could, other than you. Because I know how much love you have to give. You're loyal and honest. The best kind of man.

Just love them, please, every second of every day. Make sure they know they're loved. Make sure they feel it. Treasure every smile they share.

I'll be honest, I've sat here for hours thinking of all the things I wanted to say to you. In the beginning a hundred different demands and even threats rolled around in my mind. I even got angry, I won't deny it. The idea of any man touching the woman I love with all my heart and even more than that is hard to accept. She's mine. From the moment I first saw her, I knew she would be, and I never thought I'd be faced with the idea that she'd be with someone else.

But after the anger subsided, I was left with the demands, but not the threats. So this is me demanding that you be good to her. Sawyer is an amazing woman and she deserves an amazing life. She deserves to wake up every morning to the sounds of a man telling her that she's his world. She needs to hear that you love her, that without her you would feel empty. If you can't do those things, then I was wrong and you aren't the man for her.

But if you can, cherish every moment with her. Understand that those times are a gift, one you should feel honored to receive.

She can be difficult at times, stubborn even, but it's all part of the package. Yet you already know this. You've seen it firsthand. A piece of advice: don't ever laugh at her when she's angry, because that will only lead to a night on the couch, and trust me, sleeping by her side is so much better.

If you've chosen to love my wife, you've also chosen to love my child. This is hard for me to talk about with you, maybe even a little harder than allowing you to love Sawyer. She's felt my love, and she knows how much I adore her and how much she means to me. However, my child will never have that from me. Being a father was always one of my biggest dreams. So many nights I thought of what it would feel like to have my child look at me as if I was their hero. I dreamed of playing outside with my son, watching him grow and hearing him laugh. I dreamed about a daughter who was a mirror image of her mother, looking up at me as I leaned in to kiss her good night.

Now that gift is yours.

Please love my child. Please tell them I wanted to be their father. Make sure they know that even though I'm gone, I'm still with them. Protect them and love them more than they could have ever imagined being loved.

I mean it when I say I love you, Gage, and knowing they'll have you in their lives gives me the peace I need to move on.

Let go of the guilt I know you feel, and live. Don't be afraid to give them the amazing life I know you can. Please, brother, take care of my family.

I HAD NEVER FELT SO RAW IN MY LIFE. SO MANY thoughts and emotions ran through me that I had no idea how to deal with them all.

"I don't think he could have chosen anyone better to entrust his family to." I looked up as Luann spoke to find her and Perry standing in the doorway that led to the kitchen. Tears glistened on her cheeks as she smiled back at me. "He knew you'd love them like they needed to be loved." Her words only magnified the ache inside me. "I think deep down we all knew."

"The other letter," Perry added with a sly grin, "is just a warning to anyone else, saying he should step out of the way for his best friend, Gage." My heart lurched again and I gripped my letter just a little tighter. "He knew."

CHAPTER 33

S *awyer*

"WHERE DID THE BALL GO?" I SAT ON THE GROUND near Abby as I held my hands up, looking around on the ground before me. I couldn't hide my smile when Abigail mimicked my actions. It was adorable how her eyes widened and her little mouth formed the perfect O, her body spinning around in circles.

"Uh-oh," she said in a serious little voice as she kept looking, only now she was staring at the sky as if the ball was somehow floating above. Just when I thought she'd give up, her little gaze locked on the bright yellow ball resting against the side of the barn only a few feet from us. She beamed and giggled, and I scrunched up my nose as I tried not to cover my ears. When Abby grew excited she squealed so loud I swear it could almost break glass. And yet, instead of running toward the ball, she began jumping up and down, giggling and shrieking.

"Get it," I encouraged her, and that was all she needed. Her little legs moved so fast that she stumbled and fell to the ground before she reached her destination. I froze, thinking if I didn't make a big deal of it, she wouldn't cry, only I was wrong. Her happy squeals immediately turned into those deep screeching cries I hated to hear.

I hurried to Abigail and scooped her up. She didn't have a mark on her, but she was still scared. "It's all right, sweetheart." I rocked her from side to side. "Mommy's got you."

"Ball," she cried as she reached out, her head still buried against my chest.

"I'll get your ball," I assured her as I bent down, grabbed it up from the ground, and held it close to her side. When her little arm encircled it and her breath shuddered, I smiled because she was the sweetest thing ever, even through her tears.

"Ball," she whispered as she looked up at me, her tears slowing. Those big sad eyes and her pouting lips made my heart ache every time.

"Yeah, baby girl, that's your ball."

I squeezed her little body to my own and breathed her in. That sweet baby-fresh scent of her shampoo mixed with her lotion had such healing powers during times when I felt down.

Deciding it was time to go inside, I walked across the lawn toward the porch with Abby tucked safely to my chest. She'd long forgotten the fall and was now completely focused on the ball in her hands. I envied her. I wished I could shut off my own emotions so quickly.

As I reached the bottom of the stairs that led to my back door, I heard a car approach. When I looked up, my heart felt like it jumped into my throat, and I stumbled in surprise at the sight of Gage's silver Tahoe driving toward the house. The windows were strangely dark now. He must have tinted them since I last saw his car.

I wanted to run for the house and hide behind the safety of my closed doors, but I couldn't force my legs to move, not even when he opened his door and climbed out wearing a pair of aviators that hid those mysterious eyes of his. Not even when he offered a hesitant wave and walked toward me.

I stood there frozen as so many different emotions coursed through me—anger, frustration, and even thankfulness.

"Hey." I'd known him long enough to sense the nervousness in his voice. He was just as unsure as I was right now. "She's gotten so big," he said with a small smile as his gaze roamed over Abigail slowly.

"You missed her birthday." I hadn't meant to sound so rude, and the instant the words left my mouth, I regretted them. Sadness filled his eyes, though he attempted to hide it. I had so many unanswered questions. Part of me wanted to believe that Gage wasn't the amazing man I thought he was, but I knew better. "But the work you were doing meant something to you, so I understand the need to stay gone for so long."

My poor excuse for making things right didn't fool him. Just when I thought I'd said enough, my damn mouth kept going, digging me further into a hole. "Though a phone call would have been nice on occasion."

"I'm sorry. Yeah, it did mean something, not only to me but to the people I helped. But she means more, and so do you."

For the first time since we'd met, an uncomfortable silence settled between us. Gage and I had always found a way to make each other talk, laugh, or, hell, even cry if we needed to. But distance had grown between us, and I wasn't sure how to handle it.

Abby wiggled in my arms. "Down," she said in that determined little voice of hers. "Down, down." It was like her version of a chant.

"Wow," Gage whispered. I held her a little tighter as he stared at her, smiling. "I've missed so much," he said sadly as he brushed his fingertips against her cheek. "She looks even more like him than she did when she was born."

"I know," I agreed. "Each day I see Patrick in her more and more."

Gage kept staring at her in awe.

"I should get her inside." His gaze shifted from Abigail and connected to mine. "She's probably hungry and it's almost time for her nap."

Gage nodded and followed me into the house. My uneasiness grew at the thought that we'd be forced to talk more, because I wasn't sure what to say. My head and my heart were on two different wavelengths, and one of them was going to force my mouth to say something stupid that I couldn't take back.

"You've changed things." I peered back over my shoulder to find him looking around the kitchen in surprise.

"Just a little paint and some new curtains. Nothing major. It's amazing how much just that alone changed the feel of this place." When his eyes met mine again, I had to look away. The intensity in them made my stomach tighten with uncertainty.

He remained silent as I gathered up Abby's lunch and placed it on the tray of her high chair. The moment the food hit the tray, she went at it like a starved child. My sweet little lady had an appetite that amazed me.

Gage slid a chair up close to her, and she looked up at him as he sat. I watched in awe as he began talking to her as though he hadn't missed more than eight months of her life.

"Can I have a bite?" He leaned in close and made a *num-num* sound. "Please?"

Abby's little eyebrows lifted and she slowly moved the green bean she'd been holding toward his mouth. I was mesmerized by the interaction as he snatched the food from her fingers. Her giggle shook me from my thoughts, and I spun around, looking away as I took several slow, calming breaths, trying to hide my apprehension.

I tensed when Gage's arm brushed against mine as he stepped up beside me.

"You okay?" he asked.

"No," I said entirely too fast, and I mentally kicked myself for not lying. "Yes." I looked up to find him staring down at me, his head tilted slightly to the side. His warm, manly cologne gave me that feeling of comfort I'd grown to love whenever he was near.

"Which is it?"

I stared at him, trying to formulate an explanation for my crazy, unpredictable reaction. Instead, I looked over his features as the realization of how much I'd missed him washed over me in waves.

Bang!

I jumped and looked past him at Abby, who was slamming her sippy cup against her tray. She did that often, and I think she just liked the noise, or watching how it made her food bounce. She wasn't even looking at us.

Gage placed his hand against mine, which was still resting on the edge of the countertop. "Sawyer," he whispered, and goose bumps covered my arms.

"It's okay, you know." I wanted to stop talking, but I

couldn't. I'd been wanting to say this for a long time, and he needed to hear it now. "You made a promise to him, but it wasn't fair to you." I swallowed hard when he wrinkled his forehead. "You don't owe me anything. I'm relieving you of that promise."

Part of me wanted to scream, *Please don't accept it. Please stay and be a part of our lives. Don't leave us again.* But my throat was so tight that I couldn't speak.

He turned to face me and leaned in a little closer, making my heart ache as if it may beat out of my chest. He slowly let out a breath, yet never took his eyes from mine.

"You're right." My heart sank. "I promised him I'd watch over you both, but being here for you was never about that promise. Damn, Sawyer, I love you girls."

Yeah, of course he loved us. We were family. Well, close enough to it. I knew he cared for us. That was never a question.

"You've been a part of my life for a long time. We've shared so much over the years, but having you in my life became more real when Patrick got sick. Together, side by fucking side, we watched a man we loved more than anything fade right before us." He swallowed hard and closed his eyes for a second as if fighting against his pain. "That loss gave us a bond we wouldn't have otherwise. Not like the one we have now. I think that was what terrified me because this"—he motioned between us—"is more."

More. That one word held so many possibilities. "You're right," I confessed, "we are bonded, but you have a life to live, Gage. It's not fair for you to feel you have to place that all on hold for us."

"Don't you get it?" Gage looked over my face slowly, like he was trying to find the answers hidden somewhere within my eyes. Like he needed to know it was okay to continue speaking. "I never felt like my time with the two of you was forced or expected. It was what I wanted."

"Then why disappear? Why stay away?" My voice cracked with emotion as my vision blurred from the tears that threatened to spill over.

He hung his head as he stepped back, his hands on his hips as his shoulders rose and fell with each deep breath, like he was torn or unsure of what to say next. He seemed to be fighting an internal struggle, and it confused and worried me. "Because my guilt was eating me alive."

I watched him, waiting for clarification, or anything that would explain what was going on. When he lifted his head and his gaze locked with mine, tears glimmered in his eyes. "When I look at you now, I don't see my best friend's widow."

Watching him stare at me with such raw emotion was one of the most intense things I'd ever experienced. He was saying so much with just one look, but I was selfish and needed more. So much more.

"What do you see?" I asked, desperate to hear his answer.

"The woman I've fallen in love with." He swallowed hard, his throat bobbing. "The woman who somehow changed everything for me without even trying."

My heart raced so fast that I felt unsteady on my feet.

Gage stepped forward and I stepped back, pressing my lower back to the counter as he stood before me. Our close proximity should have scared me, but it didn't. I looked up at him and our eyes locked.

"I see someone who I know I could be happy with. Someone who will give me the life I've dreamed of. For the last nine months I've felt like I was betraying him. Like I should've been ashamed of what I've been feeling for you, and honestly I have been ashamed. It's killed me, Sawyer."

My stomach felt as if it had hollowed out and dropped to the floor.

He moved in closer, crowding me, yet I didn't stop him. I actually enjoyed how close he was getting.

"But I don't feel shame anymore, and I'm anxious to make up for everything I've missed during my time away from Abby and from you. I'm sorry I ran," he added, still watching me. "I'm sorry I stayed away so long and hid from my feelings."

"What are you saying?" I thought I knew, or at least my heart hoped I was right. But I needed to hear more to be sure that he meant what I thought he did.

"I'm saying I love you, and I love Abigail." Tears welled in my eyes as I continued to look at him. "I'm saying that though I made a promise to watch over you, that's no longer my reason for being here. I want you, and I want Abby. I want us."

"You want us?" I repeated.

Abigail squealed, banging on her tray. I was thankful she was occupied with her food for now, because I knew it wouldn't last much longer.

Gage cupped my cheek and I leaned into his touch. "I want *us*," he repeated, gently rubbing his thumb over my cheek. "I don't feel guilty anymore, because he knew, Sawyer." My eyes widened. "He knew I couldn't help but fall in love with you. How could anyone not see the beauty inside you and be weakened by it?"

I closed my eyes, willing the tears to hold off. "He told me not to be afraid to live." Yet I was afraid, because moving on meant I was letting him go, and I never wanted to do that. But Gage was the one man who would understand my forever love for Patrick. It would never come between us, he would never make me feel bad for it, and he would love Pat right alongside me. Being able to reminisce about the greatest man we'd ever known was already a bond between us. I think that alone made what Gage and I had so strong. We both loved and would always love Pat. We would also spend our lives making sure Abigail would know about her father and his love for her. Gage would be the dad she'd been robbed of, and he would ensure that Abby's memory of her daddy was never lost.

"Let's not be afraid, together."

I opened my eyes and was met with the most endearing gaze of unconditional love. I nodded in agreement, knowing that what I was about to embark upon would be a great love like the one Patrick and I had shared. But I wasn't scared. I was ready.

When Gage's lips met mine, I wrapped my hands around the back of his neck and pulled him in closer.

Our first kiss was filled with such devotion that it should've terrified me, only it excited me. I pulled back and rested my forehead against his, and we remained just like that for a few seconds, neither of us speaking.

"I think I needed time away on my own to deal with my guilt. Time to accept that what I was feeling was okay."

Though I wished he could have done that some other way, I understood. "I missed you, but in a way I think I needed you to leave." He leaned back, looking at me with confusion. "I needed to be forced to realize I could survive on my own. Yeah, there were so many times I felt like I couldn't, so many times I wanted you here, but because you weren't, I think I'm stronger now."

"I missed you too, both of you, so much." Gage draped his arms over my shoulders and pulled me in tight to his chest. "More than I could ever express. It was like part of me was missing. I woke up every day feeling as if I'd forgotten something. But now I'm whole."

I blinked past the tears that were once again pooling in my eyes. I knew exactly what he meant.

A loud squeal filled the kitchen and I laughed as Gage jerked in surprise. "She sounds like she agrees," he mumbled.

We looked back at Abby to find her smiling bright as she watched us close, holding on to her cup, which was now covered with all the food she'd smashed against it.

CHAPTER 34

G *age*

"CAN I HELP?" I ASKED AS I STEPPED UP TO Sawyer's side. She held a sleeping Abby to her chest with one arm as she tried to clear the toys Abby had been playing with from her crib.

With a gentle nod, she stepped aside and I gathered the blankets and the stuffed animals. I smiled when I picked up the pink teddy bear I'd gotten her from the hospital gift shop the day she was born.

"It's her favorite," Sawyer assured me, and call it pride or possessiveness, but that knowledge made me feel superior. "She calls it Cutie."

I looked at the two of them. Patrick's dark curls hung loosely around Abigail's face as she sucked on the two fingers that had been buried in her mouth since she'd closed her eyes. The contrast of her hair against Sawyer's blond locks that hung around her shoulders was like night and day.

I no longer felt guilty when I thought of them as mine. They were now, and not a day would go by where I would allow either of them to believe otherwise. They were now my world, my reasons for happiness, and I planned on spending the rest of my life sharing everything possible with them.

As Sawyer lowered Abby into the crib, I watched in awe. I'd never felt this kind of love before. Maybe that was wrong of me, and maybe Honor wasn't the only one to blame for our failed marriage, but I'd never felt a connection like this between her and me. This was real and raw, and it was the most intense thing I'd ever felt.

When Sawyer stepped back and I moved in to place the blanket over Abigail, that possessive feeling hit me again. I leaned over and softly placed a kissed to her forehead. "Sweet dreams, Angel," I whispered before I stepped back and allowed Sawyer to do the same.

We left the bedroom and walked toward the stairs in silence. I'd need to leave soon, but for now I needed a little more time with her, time for just the two of us. So much had taken place in the last few hours, and I guess a big part of me needed the reassurance that we were together on this journey.

When we reached the foyer at the bottom of the stairway, I took her hand and tugged just enough that she turned to face me. The only thing I wanted then was to soothe the nervousness in her eyes.

"I start back at the station tomorrow." She nodded. "It's late, I know, but part of me just wants to curl up on the couch with you and watch whatever's on TV just so I can hold you in my arms for a little longer." She nodded again. "Tell me you feel all the things I feel." Sawyer's eyes widened a little, and I was sure she was attempting to hide the reaction as she tucked her head against my shoulder. "Tell me I'm not alone in this."

"You're not alone," she whispered, but I heard her clearly. "I feel it too."

"That's all I need to know. The rest can wait." I understood why she may be hesitant, and I was patient. This was happening so fast. This time yesterday she'd had no idea where I was or what I felt for her. Now here I was, pouring out my soul to her, and she needed time to process everything.

"Do you want me to stay a little longer?" I held my breath, praying like hell that she'd say yes, but willing to accept it if she said no.

"Yes." She lifted her gaze and met mine once again. "The movie idea sounds nice."

"Okay," I said in relief.

I hooked my arm over her shoulders and walked her to the living room. Soon we were curled up on the couch, a blanket thrown over our lower halves as her head rested on my chest. I leaned forward enough that with each breath, I could smell the sweet scent of her shampoo.

I'd be lying if I said I paid any attention to the movie. But I knew exactly what it sounded like each time Sawyer took a breath and released it. I knew what it felt like to hold her, to feel her laughter against my chest. And that was all I needed to know.

I was gonna love her so hard and so deep that she'd feel like she was drowning, and nothing about that felt wrong. I was going to teach Abby all the things she needed to know about the man who loved her more than his own life, the man who helped give her life.

I was going to give them both everything Pat had ever hoped for them, and more.

THE NEXT MORNING I WOKE TO THE SOUND OF MY mother vacuuming just outside the door of the guest room I was sleeping in. I lay in bed staring at the door like she'd be able to see my annoyed look through the wood.

I really had to check with the captain about the apartment he mentioned, because living with my parents was gonna drive me fucking insane. I loved them, but I needed my space. A grown man should never, and I do mean never, move back in with his folks.

There was a knock on the door just before it burst open and Mom walked in, pushing the vacuum across the carpet. She gave me a smile, then wiggled around like the damn thing was her dance partner and they were cutting loose.

It was a good thing I had the sheet pulled up tight around my waist, because after my shower last night, I'd decided to crawl into bed forgoing a pair of boxers. My earlier thoughts of Sawyer and the effects those images had on my body were long forgotten now that my mother stood before me.

The vacuum stopped and I looked up to find her standing at the side of my bed with her hand on her hip and her eyebrow raised. She stared at me as if waiting for something.

"Um." I looked down at my side, ensuring I was in fact covered before returning her gaze. "Is there something you needed?"

"Yes. I need you to tell me how your visit with Sawyer went last night." Again she arched her brow and jutted her hip out just a little more. "Because Luann said that when you left their house, you went over there for a visit. She also told me about a certain letter you read. So before you decide to tell me you were just checking up on her, I know different. You didn't come in until after midnight last night, so I know that visit went well."

I stared at her like she'd lost her damn mind. Who knows, maybe she had.

What I found humorous—no, *strange* was a better choice of words—was that she knew when I came home. I made a mental note to contact the captain the moment my feet hit the floor.

"We talked, I played with Abigail, and then we watched a movie."

I was awarded with her stern motherly look. "And?"

"I shared what I should have shared before I left, and we're gonna see where things go."

I was met with silence.

"That's all I got for now, Ma." If I wasn't naked beneath this damn sheet, I'd leave the room to avoid her questioning stare. Something told me she understood my predicament, especially since she continued to wait for more information.

"If I had more to tell you, I would." I stared back at her, hoping she couldn't see right through my lie. Someday, hopefully soon, I'd be able to confess the love I felt for Sawyer and Abigail freely without fear of what people would think, but for now I'd chosen to keep what was developing between us to myself.

"You need to have those girls over for dinner." She moved her hand from her hip and pushed the vacuum toward the door. "Because I know damn well there's more to this story than what you're sharing. Give me five minutes with her and I'll have the two of you living the life you're meant to."

She stepped out into the hallway and pulled the door shut behind her, leaving me feeling bulldozed.

I leaned over and snatched my phone from the nightstand, then sent the captain a message. I needed that apartment.

CHAPTER 35

S awyer

"SHE'S FIGHTING ANOTHER EAR INFECTION." I leaned over and placed a kiss on Abby's forehead. "It's the third one in the last four months."

"What does her doctor say?" Rachel sat in the chair a few feet away looking at Abigail with concern.

"They mentioned the possibility of putting in tubes." I smoothed the hair from my little girl's forehead. "Is it wrong to be terrified at the idea of her going under?" I looked up at Rachel for reassurance. "It's just a scary thought, and I know it's crazy and that things like this take place almost daily, but...."

I was being ridiculous. I already knew I was.

"Everything will be okay." She gave me that motherly soothing look I'd realized lately that I cherished. Over the last year I'd turned to Rachel countless times for advice about

Abby and being a mother. "Maybe she'll outgrow it, but if she doesn't and there's a need for tubes, it'll still be all right."

I nodded, though I was still unsure.

"Now, why don't you get going. She's asleep, and I know that Gage is expecting you."

I remained seated on the floor next the couch where Abby slept as I combed my fingers through her hair. "She's had her Motrin but—"

"I know. If she wakes and still seems fine, give her Tylenol before she starts showing signs of pain. Don't worry, dear. I know what I'm doing. Now get going, and please don't worry. I'll call if I need anything."

"I'll call you to check in," I said as I leaned in to give Abby one more kiss. When I looked up at Rachel, she was smiling back at me as if she already knew I'd call and text often. "I won't be long."

"Take all the time you need." She practically shoved me out the door.

During the drive across town from Rachel's to Gage's apartment, I thought of turning back around. Leaving Abigail was hard enough, but it was even harder when she wasn't feeling well.

My pulse quickened as I pulled up outside the four-unit building. Gage was walking into the lower unit to the left, carrying a box. His shirt was off and hanging from his back pocket. Two other men followed, carrying a couch, and they tilted it to get it through the door. They wore bright orange shirts with a logo on them that matched the one on their moving truck. The words *Southern Movers* across the back indicated the company they worked for.

After they got the couch through, Gage reappeared in the doorway and planted his hands on his hips. Taking a deep breath, I opened the car door. The movement gained his attention and he walked over.

"Hey," he said as he stepped up and leaned in to kiss me softly. "Sorry I'm sweaty." He moved back, creating space once again. "Where's Abby?" He looked over my shoulder at the empty car seat in the back.

"Ear infection," I said, and concern washed over his face, making my heart ache. "She's with Rachel for a few hours. She fell asleep after I gave her some meds, so she'll be fine."

He still didn't look convinced. "We can do this another time."

"Nope," I said, though my mind agreed. "You asked me to help you make this place look as though you actually live here instead of just renting it for the time being. So that's what I'm here to do." I stepped forward and gave him my best smile. "Show me the way."

He allowed me to pass, then wrapped his arms around me from behind after I'd only moved a few feet. I squealed when his chest pressed tightly to my back and he kissed the side of my neck. "Thank you for coming," he whispered before kissing up toward my ear. "I was hoping to have you and Abby over tonight for pizza maybe."

I looked back over my shoulder at him. He was so cute with that hopeful look in his eyes. "Maybe she'll feel up to it. We'll see."

I remember the way I felt when I'd first met Pat. The excitement and newness of those first steps in a relationship. The nerves and the fear of something messing it up were all so unpredictable. But it was different with Gage. We'd known each other for so long, and the comfortable feeling I'd get from his touch that made every move he made and every word he spoke feel so real. Falling in love and getting to know someone while worrying about what to do or say wasn't something we had to deal with. We already had the attachment that generally takes weeks into a new relationship to develop.

Hand in hand, he led me to the apartment and we stepped aside as the two men exited the front door. They nodded as they walked to their truck for the next piece of furniture.

"Was easier to let them load and unload," Gage said before pulling me inside.

The apartment had a small living room and kitchen separated by a bit of space for a table. The two doors at the back of the living room led, I assumed, to the bedroom and bathroom.

"It's small but I don't need much space." He leaned against one of the doors as I did a full turn in the center of the room. "And I had to get out of my parents' house."

I arched a brow and he laughed.

"My mother, God love her, she hovers." It was now my turn to laugh. "I'd had enough the moment she walked into the guest room carrying a basket with all my clothes, telling me she thought I should wear the loose boxers my father wears instead of tight boxer briefs."

My laughter grew heavier.

"She even bought me a package of plaid ones and said I should give them a try."

"And did you?" I asked as he stared at me with his arms crossed over his bare chest. He unlinked them and reached for the waistband of his pants, then pushed them down his trim waist just enough to show the band around the top of his boxers that displayed the words *Calvin Klein*. "Nope," he said, and I looked up at his knowing smirk. "I'll stick with these."

"Good choice." My voice came out in a hoarse whisper as I realized the effect that small movement had on me. Gage was a fit and appealing man.

CHAPTER 36

G *age*

"WHAT'S THE HURRY?" ERIC STEPPED IN FRONT OF me before I could hurry past him. "Got a hot date?" He sidestepped and blocked me when I attempted to go left.

"Yeah, actually I do."

He arched his brow and got out of my way. I knew that people would have opinions about Sawyer and me being together. Some would assume we had something going on all this time, or possibly even before Patrick passed. She and I had talked about this over and over and had finally agreed that our families were the only ones who needed to know. People who looked down on our decision or thought the worst of us didn't belong in our lives.

"And?"

"Sawyer," I said without feeling an ounce of guilt. "I'm taking Sawyer out to dinner."

I weighed Eric's expression—the surprised lift of his brows, the way his mouth hung open.

"That's good, man." Eric slapped my shoulder and gave it a firm squeeze. "Real good."

I was a little surprised. I guess I expected more resistance. Eric may not have been as close to Patrick as I'd been, but he still knew him. We were all friends.

"Yeah," I said because honestly I didn't know what else to say.

"I think he'd approve," Eric added as he stepped back, and my chest tightened. "Face it, man, he trusted you more than anyone else."

I left the station feeling good about the night. This would be our first official date, or whatever, and Willow had insisted on babysitting Abby. I was still shocked at how everyone in our families had accepted this, as if they'd already approved of us being together and had only been waiting on us to catch up with the idea. It was surreal.

After a quick shower, I threw on my clothes and practically jogged out of the house. Fuck, I felt like a kid again. My body hummed with excitement as I drove up the drive toward Sawyer's. The porch light was on, and the blind moved on the sidelite just to the left of the door, which led me to believe she'd been watching and waiting.

As I walked up the porch steps, the front door open and I froze, unable to move any farther.

"Damn," I mumbled, and she grinned so wide it made me chuckle. "Sorry, but—" I shook my head. What the fuck was wrong with me? I was tripping over my words. "You look amazing."

"Thank you." Her smile grew and it made my heart race. Before I could stop myself, I went to her and cupped her face, pulling her lips to mine. When she sighed I slid my tongue along the seam and took advantage of the moment they parted.

"You're beautiful," I whispered before I kissed her again, not giving her a second to respond. "I've been looking forward to tonight since the moment you said yes."

"Me too," she confessed as we rested our foreheads together while I tried to slow my racing heart.

"Did Willow already pick up Abby?"

When she nodded I felt a pang of disappointment at not being able to step inside and give her a hug. "Well then, I guess we can take off. Are you ready?"

She nodded and I linked my fingers with hers and led her down the stairs to the passenger side of my Tahoe. When she was buckled up, I leaned in to steal another quick kiss before closing the door and hurrying around to the other side. I couldn't stop myself from linking our fingers again and resting them on her thigh. She smiled brightly as she looked down at our joined hands while I backed out of the drive.

When I'd asked her three days ago where she wanted to go for dinner, I chuckled at her answer: Texas Roadhouse. Sawyer was simple, and I loved it. She felt no need to even attempt to impress anyone around her.

A few familiar faces glanced at us as the waitress led us toward our booth. It may have been related to the fact I was still firmly holding her hand, but I wasn't willing to let go and she didn't seem willing to, either. When we slid into the booth, she made sure to slide all the way to the end, opening up the space next to her, and I followed right behind.

"They all gotta get used to it sometime, right?" Those big beautiful blue eyes stared up at me in hope and I couldn't help but close the distance between us and press a gentle kiss to her lips.

"Yes, they do," I assured her.

Throughout dinner we laughed and things felt natural.

There was no shying away from the topic of Patrick—hell, we talked about him freely and smiled as we remembered everything the three of us had shared. Neither of us cared about the curious glances or even those who gaped in shock.

I paid the check and we stood, then I wrapped my arm over her shoulders. Side by side we walked out of the restaurant and headed toward the truck.

"Gage?"

Sawyer paused as a woman said my name. I didn't have to look to know it was Honor. I'd spent long enough with her to recognize her voice.

"It is you." I turned back to the restaurant to find Honor walking toward us while leaving behind a man near the restaurant doors who looked old enough to be her father. His hair was silver, his eyes were wrinkled around the edges, and from the looks of his suit and Rolex, I'd say she'd finally found someone to support her expensive spending habits and tastes.

"When did you get back in town?" She threw her arms over my shoulders as if we were longtime friends and not ex-husband and wife.

She didn't even acknowledge Sawyer.

"About a week ago," I replied before pulling Sawyer to my side.

Honor raked her eyes over Sawyer from head to toe. "Well, you should've called."

It was all an act. I'd recognized it immediately.

"Why would I?" She flinched. "We're divorced, and even before that there were days, weeks even, that we didn't talk. Hell, we lived in the same house and rarely saw one another." Honor looked back over her shoulder at the guy, who watched us closely. "Let's not pretend we're anything more than two people who made a mistake when we thought we were right for each other."

"So did the two of you always have something going on behind our backs?"

Sawyer stepped forward, but I took her arm to stop her.

"Let's not do this, because I think you already know the answer to that, and you're only gonna further embarrass yourself in front of your friend." Part of me was pissed at the insinuation that I would have cheated on her, and with my dying best friend's wife no less. But I knew her well enough to know she understood how farfetched that was. "The only blessings we needed were Patrick's and our families', and we got those. Nothing else matters, Honor. Nothing."

We stood there staring back at one another as I waited to see if she'd say anything more. When she didn't and her shoulders sagged, I looked up at the man who still waited for her to come back. "You have a nice night."

He offered a hesitant wave, and Sawyer and I walked to my SUV.

"What did you mean when you said we got Patrick's blessing?"

I paused with my hand on the handle of the passenger door and looked over at Sawyer to find her watching me closely. "Back there you said Pat's blessing and our families' was all we needed, and we'd gotten that. I understand that we got our families' approval, but Pat's?"

I always knew that someday I would show her the letter Patrick left for me. I just didn't imagine it would be tonight.

"He left me a letter." Her eyes wrinkled in confusion. "Perry had two, actually: one for any man you one day decided to move forward with, and one for me."

Her eyes filled with tears and I reached for her, but she held up her hand, making my heart lurch. "What did it say?"

"Just that—"

"No, I wanna read it."

I wondered if this was an appropriate time or place to

have this discussion. I thought about convincing her to allow me to drive her back to the house, where we could talk about this in private, but I knew that wouldn't happen. I could see the determination in her eyes, and when Sawyer got that way, nothing would change her mind.

"I *need* to read it." Her voice cracked with emotion even as she tried to control it. I understood her need to know now; I'd felt the same the moment I knew the letter existed. These were Pat's words, and the longing to know what he felt was too powerful to ignore. I stepped back and reached into my back pocket for my wallet. Her gaze was practically glued to my movements as I unfolded the worn leather and took out the letter I'd carried with me every day since Perry handed it to me. I'd fully intended to put it somewhere safe, but during my move I was fearful of misplacing it, and my wallet seemed like a safe place at the time.

I handed it to her and she unfolded it carefully, as if it was the most precious thing she'd ever held. I understood, because to me, it was. That letter was Patrick's permission for me to love Sawyer. It was the greatest gift he'd ever given me.

Her eyes shifted from side to side as she read each line. Tears formed in them before slowly running along her cheeks. I wanted to take her in my arms and soothe her, only I knew she needed this so I fought the urge. Watching her fall apart and not doing a damn thing was one of the hardest things I'd ever done.

"He knew," she whispered without looking up from the paper. "How?"

"I don't know." I'd asked myself that same question so many times. "He just did."

Sawyer let out a slow, steady breath before carefully refolding the letter. When she held it out to me, I felt like I'd been kicked in the stomach because she wouldn't look at me.

Instead, she focused on the empty space between us and twisted her hands after I took the paper. Her gaze shifted to my hands as I placed the letter in my wallet and put it in my back pocket.

"Sawyer," I said, though I wasn't exactly sure what I intended to say after. It was more of a plea to gain her attention.

"Can you just take me home?"

I nodded, though she was looking down again as she took in one deep breath after another.

I'd give her time to process this, but there was no way in hell I'd let her go.

CHAPTER 37

S *awyer*

"MOMMY!" I BENT DOWN JUST IN TIME TO CATCH Abigail as she dove toward me. She was still wearing her Cinderella pajamas and her hair was in pigtails, but one hung a lot lower than the other.

Her giggles as I lifted her and kissed her cheek eased my sadness a bit.

"So how was last night?" Willow asked eagerly, gaining my full attention. I couldn't help laughing as I saw that she, too, wore Cinderella pajamas, though they were a more grown-up version of Abby's.

"What the hell are you wearing?"

She looked down and rocked back on her heels as if taking herself completely in before looking back at me. "Princess pajamas." Her casual tone and the way she wrinkled her brows and nose made me laugh even more. "What's wrong with 'em?"

"Nothing," I assured her, "nothing at all."

Instead of plying me with further questions, she shrugged and spun around, then walked toward her small kitchen. "So are you gonna tell me about your night or do I need to call up my new BFF, Gage, and get the details?"

Abby began wriggling, so I lowered her to the ground so she could go back to watching cartoons. I moved up to the counter separating the kitchen and living room. "Did you read the letter?"

Willow looked back over her shoulder as she lowered the coffeepot back to the base. "What letter?"

"The one Patrick wrote for Gage." She averted her gaze and lifted both steaming cups from the counter, then moved over and placed one before me. "The letter your dad had, the one Gage now has in his wallet."

She didn't have to answer me. I could see the answer in her eyes.

"Do you think it's our obligation?" Willow tilted her head and stared at me in confusion. "Like maybe he feels as if he has to care for us; like everyone expects him to love us now that they know what Patrick hoped for."

"Do you honestly believe that?" Willow placed her coffee on the counter and pressed her palms on the granite surface. "Because if you actually say yes, you might just piss me off."

"I just keep thinking—"

"Stop." Her stern tone surprised me. "Gage spent months trying to ignore his feelings for you. He went to Arizona to put distance between you, hoping he'd be able to clear his head and forget what he felt. That man cried and grew angry with himself over and over, feeling ashamed of loving you for months, Sawyer." She kept her voice low, but I heard the intensity in it. " Patrick's letter was what finally gave him clarity. It allowed him to accept what he'd felt for you and understand that those feelings were okay. Don't you dare try to make what he's feeling out to be some repayment to my brother."

Tears welled in my eyes because I knew she was right. God, I knew that.

"Patrick loved you so much, and all he wanted was for you to find that kind of love again. He knew that Gage was the one who could give you that. He knew before any of us did. Don't push him away, Sawyer. Let him love you."

"I want to," I confessed. "I'm just scared."

"Of what?" Willow moved around the counter and stepped up to my side.

"Forgetting him." My vision blurred with tears. "Sometimes I wake up and I can still see him so clearly. I can imagine the way his eyes wrinkled when he grinned. Or I can hear his laughter when I'd go on one of my rambles and he was unable to hold it back." My heart ached with each confession. "When I walk into a room, I swear I can sometimes still smell him, like he's there waiting for me. I've even looked around like I'd actually find him watching television or pouring a cup of coffee."

"And all of that is okay."

"I care about Gage so much, and I may even love him." I paused, knowing I was lying to myself. "I do love him," I corrected. "But I'm scared that if I move forward, if I allow myself to love Gage the way I want to, that I'll forget all the things about Patrick that I adored."

Willow pulled me into a hug and I let go of my pain and sobbed on her shoulder in a mixture of sadness and confusion.

"You'll never forget," she whispered. "Gage wouldn't let you. We both know he would never try to replace Pat. He'd ensure that Pat stayed a big part of all your lives."

After a much-needed cry, I moved back and sat on the barstool only a few feet away. Abigail was still watching TV, completely oblivious to what had taken place only seconds ago. Willow sat on a stool next to me, and a million things rolled around in my mind, but one stuck out above all others.

"Do you think you could watch Abigail for a little longer?" I looked up as she took a sip of coffee. "I think I owe someone an explanation as to why I grew so cold last night."

"Of course," Willow said as she lowered her cup. "I promised her pancakes and eggs." She grinned wide. "There may have been a mention of chocolate chips too."

I arched a brow at her and she laughed.

"What? Isn't it in the aunt handbook that I should spoil my one and only niece every single chance I get?"

"Yeah," I replied, feeling as if it was a little easier to smile now that my fears had been soothed. "It sure is."

MY NERVES WERE GOING CRAZY AND MY STOMACH knotted as I took each step.

I'd sat in my car for the last few minutes watching Gage and his father move around the car in the garage. They'd disappear under the hood before reappearing again. When I'd realized that no amount of rehearsing would give me the exact words to say, I gave up trying to think of them and climbed out. When the door shut and I turned toward the house, Gage stood with his hand on the fender, staring at me. I couldn't quite tell if he was happy to see me or confused by my arrival.

With each step I took, he moved toward me, and we met in the middle of his parents' driveway. He stood with his hands pushed deep in his front pockets and I twisted my own nervously before me.

"Everything okay?" he finally asked, and all I could do was shake my head. "Sawyer, what's wrong?"

"I'm sorry." Fear flashed in his eyes as he pulled his hands from his pockets and reached for me. He held my waist as if he was scared to let go; worried I'd run.

"About last night, I handled it wrong and I'm sorry." He shook his head as if he disagreed. "Yes, I did. I shouldn't have closed off my feelings. I should've shared them."

"So share them now." I looked over his shoulder at the garage and found it was now empty. "He went inside."

I took a deep breath before looking back up at Gage. "I love you too," I said in a rush, but I had to get it out. I had to beat my fear. Gage smiled, which admittedly wasn't the reaction I'd imagined. "I know I didn't say it back that day, but it didn't mean that I didn't love you. I was just fearing that connection."

"Why?" he asked, moving in closer as he pulled me to him. The warmth of his chest against mine gave me comfort. "Tell me what you're scared of."

"Forgetting." The tears that came each time I admitted this fear returned. "I wanna move forward, I wanna live, but I'm scared if I do, I'm agreeing to forget him, and that's the scary part."

Gage released my waist and cupped my face. With my chin tilted upward, I looked into his eyes and saw the love there. "I'll never let you forget him." It was a promise. "He'll always be part of us, Sawyer. He'll be the one we thank every day when we wake up next to each other. He'll be the father I tell stories to about Abby each night when we put her to bed. I promise you there will never be a time when Patrick isn't a part of our day."

"I know, but that fear is still there. No matter how hard I try to soothe it, it's there."

"Then we'll take it one day at a time." Gage skimmed his

thumb over my jaw, his eyes holding the promise of every-thing he'd said. "You let me show you each day that I mean what I say. Let me be the man I know I can be for you and for Abby. And let me be the man Patrick knew I was before I even did."

I closed my eyes as a tear ran over my cheek.

Gage pressed his lips over the path of my tears as if to kiss them away. "Don't push me away, Sawyer, please," he whispered. "I need you."

I shuddered with the impact of his words and wrapped my arms around him to hold him closer. "I need you too," I confessed, and for the first time since I'd read the letter Patrick had left Gage, that didn't frighten me.

CHAPTER 38

G *age*

I KNOCKED LIGHTLY ON THE DOOR BEFORE
twisting the knob and finding it unlocked. Making a mental
note to lecture Sawyer about safety precautions, I was met
with soft music.

I walked to the kitchen, where I paused just outside the
entryway and listened to Sawyer singing along. It was a
familiar song, one I'd heard on the radio probably a hundred
times without paying much attention to the words or their
meaning. Now I closed my eyes and just listened to her
sing them.

The song was about feeling lost and learning to love
again; moving on and remembering what it felt like to feel
safe. The lyrics made me feel an ache in my chest, one that
was related to the pain I knew she felt and to my desire to
heal her and make her feel whole again.

Even before I fell for her, Sawyer's tears had always been like a knife to my chest.

I stepped through the doorway and watched in awe as she swayed from side to side, holding Abigail against her chest. One tiny leg was thrown over each side of her waist, and a mess of black curls lay over her left shoulder. As if hearing her singing such a heartfelt song wasn't enough, this sight made me feel raw, and the unconditional love I felt for not only Sawyer but Abby hit me strong.

I'd heard about things bringing a grown man to his knees, yet until that moment I never really understood how something so simple could do just that. But the two of them made my legs weak. Fuck, I never thought it was possible to feel so wrapped up in anyone, let alone two people. These two girls were my world. They were my life, the life I'd never imagined having but had been blessed with. And here they were before me, to love and protect.

I stepped up behind Sawyer and wrapped them both in my arms. She didn't pull away as my chin rested upon her shoulder. From this angle I could see them both, along with the contour of Sawyer's cheek as it rolled into her jaw, and the most kissable neck I'd ever been within inches of. Unable to control the urge, I pressed a soft kiss where it met her chest.

I smiled against her before moving back just enough to watch Abby. Her eyes were closed and her little lips were puckered, only a small opening allowing each breath to escape. Every time I looked at her, her resemblance to Patrick hit me hard. And every time I saw it, I wished he could too. He would have adored her and cherished her.

We remained just like this for song after song. It was almost overwhelming to know that the girls I held now were my key to a happiness I'd never imagined. A love that was so deep and strong it made me feel weak.

"Can we just take a little time-out to miss him together?" I asked, knowing the reaction I'd get but feeling as if I had to ask. I never wanted her to feel like we couldn't love Patrick and wish that things had turned out differently.

"Yes." Her hoarse voice made my throat ache and I tried to swallow past the pain. "Me missing him doesn't mean I don't thank God for you. Sometimes I still feel guilty for being happy. It's the strangest feeling, this back-and-forth tug of emotions. I sometimes wish he was here and that things were different, then I find myself thinking if that had happened, I wouldn't have you the way that I do now. Then I hurt all over again but for different reasons." She took in a shuddering breath. "Then I just feel stupid because no amount of wishing can change the past." She turned in my arms and looked at me with fresh tears in her eyes. "I'm thankful for you, Gage. I am, and I never want you to think you're any less important to me than—"

I pulled her to me and pressed my lips to hers. I didn't regret what was taking place between us, and I never would. She was right; we couldn't change anything that had happened. We would always love Patrick, but she was my future and together we'd heal. I knew in the end that our grief would only make us stronger.

"Love you," I whispered against her lips as she took another shuddering breath. "I got you, my beautiful angel. No guilt." I leaned my forehead against hers and we took one calming breath after another. "We'll do this together, one day at a time."

She nodded and I again wrapped my arms around them as Sawyer rested her head upon my chest. With Abigail cocooned between us, we swayed along to the radio.

"WE HAVE A HOUSE FIRE ON CONNOR DRIVE." ERIC tossed me my helmet as I rounded the back of the truck while the alarms echoed throughout the loading dock. "Kitchen," he added as he climbed onto the truck, "most likely someone forgot about something on the stove."

Things had been slow today, and the time for a shift change was nearing, but the alarm now had us all hyped and ready.

I hadn't always dreamed of being a fireman. Hell, when I was young I wanted to be Iron Man and save the world. Then one day, I think I was in fifth grade, a firefighter came to my school, and we all sat around in the gymnasium as he talked about his job. I still remember the stories he shared about those he'd saved and the lives he'd impacted throughout the years.

I can still see the look in my father's eyes when I told him I wanted to rescue people. I wanted to have someone look at me the way I looked at that firefighter and feel the same things I felt about him. He was heroic, and to me that was the closest thing to being someone who could save the world.

My childhood dream became my reality and I loved it.

Smoke poured out a small window in the back as we pulled up to the address. An elderly woman stood on the front lawn waving her hands high in the air.

"I can't find Elmer," she cried in near hysterics as she ran out to meet us, pointing toward the house. "He was there, then he wasn't, and I've looked everywhere."

"There's someone inside, ma'am?" I asked as I looked past her at the house, my heart racing.

"Yes, Elmer. He gets spooked easily, and when the fire alarm went off, he ran."

"Eric, there's a man inside," I hollered as he moved toward the front door. "Elmer is his name."

"Elmer's not a man." I gave the woman a curious look. "He's my cat."

I looked up to see Curtis walking out the front door carrying a black-and-white cat, and the woman's expression lit up like a Christmas tree. "Oh, thank you." She took Elmer from Curt. "Thank you for saving my baby."

It did end up being a small kitchen fire, and though it did cause damage, it was easily extinguished. On the drive back to the station, we had fun harassing Curtis, calling him the Cat Whisperer and several other things. When he started eating it up and insisted that from now on we should refer to him as the man pussy runs to and not the man pussy runs away from, the joke was no longer fun.

CHAPTER 39

S*awyer*

I LAID THE RED ROSE AGAINST THE TOMBSTONE before sitting on the grass beside it. Leaning my back against the granite, I looked at the bright sky and smiled.

Each day got a little easier. I missed Patrick a little less, and though it made me sad, I knew it was part of healing. I'd always remember every moment we shared and the love I'd forever hold close, but I knew this was what he'd want for me. He'd want me to live on as he'd told me so many times before.

Each Sunday after I dropped Abby off with Luann and Pete for a few hours, I came here for a while. Sometimes I'd share the stories of our daughter and how each day her cute little personality developed even more. Gage had a part in that, because the more time she spent with him, the more I saw him in her too. He loved her, and seeing them together was bitter-sweet. She saw him as her father, and I'd try to remember that Patrick would be okay with that. In his absence Gage was the runner-up for the man who loved her most. He would teach her all the things Patrick would have, had he been here to.

"I'm happy, Pat," I whispered to the sky. "I miss you so much it still hurts, but he makes things better. For the first time since I found out you were sick, I feel like smiling is a little easier. I have Gage to thank for that, and you too." I took a deep breath. "You brought him into my life."

I wasn't sure just how much time passed as I looked at the sky and listened to the wind in the trees, but I left the cemetery feeling a peace I hadn't when I'd arrived.

I drove across town to the café I used to visit often and grabbed two cups of coffee, then drove a few streets over and parked outside the fire station.

As I climbed from the car and walked to the big garage door, I heard laughter from inside.

"That's fucking cold," Gage said just before another man's squeal echoed through the open space. "Told you it was cold, you asshole."

I peeked in, hoping that whatever the two were doing, they wouldn't decide to do to me. I could hear water hitting the concrete and firetruck, and being drenched with a cold stream of water didn't sound too appealing. I found Gage and another guy standing next to the fire truck, both shirtless and dripping.

"So is this what our tax dollars pay for?" They turned to face me and I smiled. "Water fights?"

"Why, wanna join us?" Gage walked toward me with a mischievous grin that made my heart skip a beat. Those leering eyes and that smile were definitely a little dangerous to a girl's libido.

"I think I'll pass." My voice sounded breathy and his grin grew even wider as I scanned over his body.

He wrapped his arm around my waist and pulled me tightly against him, and I squealed when the cool water on his chest soaked through my T-shirt. "That is so cold." Chills broke out over my arms and neck.

"This is a nice surprise."

I held up the two coffee cups. "I thought I'd invade your space."

"I like when you make my choices like that." He licked his lower lip as he brought his face in just a little closer to mine. "But I think I'd rather taste these." He took my mouth in a slow, teasing kiss.

I'd completely forgotten we weren't alone until the sound of someone clearing their throat broke my trance. I pulled back quickly, my eyes widening in embarrassment as I realized someone had been watching this.

Gage's grin widened. "Curt, this is Sawyer, my girl." Instead of turning around to look at the guy, he continued to watch me. Hearing him call me his girl did something to me, something strange and new and exciting. "Sawyer, this is Curt." He jerked his head in the man's direction.

Peeking over Gage's bare shoulder, I offered Curt a smile.

"So you're the Sawyer I've been hearing so much about." Now I was interested. "Granted, most of the guys knew of you already, but I've never had the pleasure. I'll be honest." Curt crossed his arms over his chest and leaned against the fire truck. "I thought for sure they were all in on this game of the phantom girl."

"Phantom girl?" I looked from him to Gage, and Gage chuckled as he hung his head.

"Yeah," Curt added, regaining my attention. "The way this guy talks about you, I was convinced there was no way you actually existed."

Arching my brow, I looked at Gage for clarification.

"Guy's just jealous," he offered with a shrug. "I got the only good one and he's stuck still searching."

I stood in silence as they laughed and teased each other. It was yet another moment where I felt lighter. Another sign that life did move on, whether you wanted it to or not.

It was strange to look at Gage and see a future with him. I'd thought the chance of any happiness outside of Abigail couldn't possibly be out there for me.

But I was wrong. Gage had proven me wrong, and it made me love him even more.

CHAPTER 40

G *age*

"More." Abby repeated the word as she bounced on my stomach. She sat with one little leg on each side, holding her arms out as she waited for me to once again lift her high in the air over me and move her around from side to side.

"More," she squealed just before I scooped her up and raised her. She giggled, kicking her legs.

"You do realize now that you've started this, she'll never let you stop?"

I looked to the left to find Sawyer leaning against the doorway to the kitchen with her arms crossed over her chest and her lips pursed. I'd gotten so used to kissing those lips over the past few weeks that it was hard to withstand a day without them. I hated my nightshifts at the station.

"I knew that when I started," I assured her with a wink

just before I lowered a happy little girl back to my chest. She immediately began chanting for more.

Out of the corner of my eye, I watched Sawyer move in closer and sink beside me onto the floor. "Abigail," she tried to gain the attention of the determined little lady who clawed at me, saying her new favorite word. "Watch Mommy." Sawyer leaned in, and just when I was about to ask what she was doing, she rested her head against my chest. I still choked up every time she did that. And as if that wasn't enough to weaken any man, I was fucking lost when Abby laid her head opposite Sawyer's.

The tightening in my chest threatened my control as I held them. I watched as they stared at one another, and soon Abby's eyelids drooped.

When her breaths evened out and her body grew heavy, I knew she was asleep. I remained silent as I watched Sawyer stare at her now-sleeping daughter. It was another one of those beautiful moments I knew I would never forget.

"I love you," I whispered, gaining Sawyer's full attention as she tilted her head back a little more, allowing me to see all of her face.

"And I love you."

That had quickly become something we'd say often throughout every day.

"She loves you too." Sawyer placed her hand on Abby's back just over mine.

For a few seconds we remained just like that. It was enough. Hell, it was everything to be allowed to share moments like these.

"Stay." I looked back at Sawyer and found her watching me with hopeful eyes. "I want you to."

My heart sped like a teenager's at the mention of spending the night. We'd not crossed that line yet, but at the pace we were going, it felt right and it was what we both needed.

"Are you sure?"

"Yes," she reassured me, "I'm sure."

I FOLLOWED SAWYER INTO THE BEDROOM, HER hand in mine as she led the way. I shook with the adrenaline coursing through me. She paused at the side of the bed, and her shoulders rose and fell with a deep breath before she turned to face me.

"There's no rush," I assured her as she stepped closer and placed her hands on my chest.

"I know," she replied with a smile that soothed my worries. "I'm not rushing, I'm just feeling."

I knew exactly what she meant because I was feeling it too.

She slowly lowered her hands and gathered the hem of her shirt, then lifted it up and over her head. My breath rushed out and I withheld the moan boiling inside me.

I was mesmerized as she unhooked her bra and glided each strap over her shoulders and down her arms. Only when the silk garment fell to her feet did I let out a groan. My reaction triggered a smile from her just before she moved closer, this time lifting my shirt up and over my head.

I allowed her to lead, because quite frankly I found her courage sexy.

When my own shirt was lying on the floor with hers, she pressed a kiss over my heart and I lost a small bit of control. I gripped her waist and lifted her feet from the floor, bringing her body flush to mine. Without pause I placed her on the bed, then crawled on after her and held her tight.

With my lips pressed to hers, I moved my tongue over

them and swallowed the moan that escaped her. "You're perfect," I said, only moving away for a second before going back for more. I glided my palm over her hip, then along her waist and traced the contour of her breast, and smiled when she arched her back and pushed herself against me.

"Please don't stop."

Part of me wanted to assure her I had no intention of stopping, but I showed her instead. I kissed along her jaw and the side of her neck, and with each flick of my tongue, she gripped my shoulders tighter. Her nipple tightened against my chest and I shook with anticipation as I descended and covered her left one with my lips. With a gentle suck, she ignited and shifted her hips upward, almost begging for more.

With each kiss and touch, she whimpered and made needy little moans that made it hard to not grab her and take what my body demanded. Damn, I was a ball of lust, but I wanted to take my time memorizing each curve of her body.

When I reached her waist, I carefully unfastened her jeans as I watched for her reaction. When I slowly slid them down her hips, she egged me on, wiggling from side to side as if to speed up the process. The urgency of her movements intrigued me.

"In a hurry?" I said with a smile, and she gave me a quick nod. Apparently I wasn't the only one fighting for control. To taunt her and give myself the satisfaction of knowing just how much she wanted this, I slowly unfastened my own jeans. Just before I lowered them, I reached inside my pocket and retrieved the condom.

She watched, her chest rising and falling with each needy breath, and I realized that prolonging this wasn't only torturing her. Fuck, I was so hard it actually hurt when my jeans slid over my erection.

"Please," Sawyer pleaded as she lifted her legs and pulled

of her panties before lowering her legs once more and parting them.

I had never wanted a woman more than the one splayed out before me. She was perfection, so beautiful and ready.

I yanked off my jeans and boxers and tossed them to the floor. I lifted the condom to my lips and tore the packet open, then rolled it over my cock. When I looked up we were both focused on my movements.

I wanted to worship her, taste her, and touch every inch of her, but that would have to wait. We both needed this; we needed to feel the other. We had forever for the rest.

As I positioned myself before her, I looked her in the eyes and silently asked for one more sign that this was what she wanted. She nodded as she reached out for me, and with slow and careful movements, I moved forward and slid inside her. My eyes rolled back as I held my breath and tried to hold on to my last ounce of control.

But it was lost the second she whispered, "Gage."

I gripped her face in one hand and braced the weight of my body on the other as I began to move. Her eyes locked with mine, and we shared so much between us with just that look. Fuck, I felt so many things all at once that I thought I was going to explode.

"I love you," she whispered, as if she knew in that moment that I needed to hear it. I could feel myself slipping, and those three words pulled me back to the present.

"I love you, so much."

My movements slowed and I watched as she fell into the pleasure I was giving her. Her walls tightened around me and she felt so good, so perfect.

"Let go," I whispered, encouraging her to give in to what she was feeling. "Show me what I do to you."

I could sense the way her body reacted to my encouraging

words, almost like a trigger. Her fingers dug into my flesh as her back arched and her hips jerked.

"Let me feel you, baby." I continued feeling the powerful rush each twitch of her body gave me, and the way it tightened around me as her pleasure grew. I was like a starving man, needing—no, demanding—her release.

"Yes," she cried out as her legs tightened around my waist and she thrust her hips upward to meet mine. "Oh my God, yes."

I let her seek what she needed while I watched her face closely. The crease of her forehead, the way she bit her lower lip hard. She was even more beautiful when she lost control.

CHAPTER 41

S *awyer*

I FELT LIKE I HAD A FEVER AS I ATTEMPTED TO ROLL to my side, only to find I was pinned beneath something heavy and unwilling to move.

I opened one eye and found not only the thing holding me in place, but the source of the heat. Gage was like a blanket, one that wrapped around me so tightly I wasn't sure where he ended and I began.

"Gage." I nudged his shoulder, and his displeased groan made me laugh. "You need to move." I nudged him again and he squeezed me tighter.

"Stop pushing, woman," he mumbled with his eyes still closed. "I'm comfortable and you're trapped. We both already know you're not winning, so stop trying and lie still already."

I lay there for a few seconds trying to come up with anything that would prove him wrong. A memory popped into my mind that I knew would definitely be useful in my current situation. I carefully repositioned my body, as if I was actually agreeing, then glided my hand along his shoulder and along his back, then shifted it to his side and attacked.

I had never in my life heard any man make the noise that ripped out of Gage. It reminded me of the way Abigail squealed when she was excited. His large frame tensed as he curled away from me, and within seconds he was standing on the opposite side of the bed, his chest rising and falling as he stared at me.

I shrugged, still trying to hold back my laughter. "Thought you said I wouldn't win?" I was playing with fire, but it was just too satisfying to stop. "Looks like I won this round." I slid back and stood opposite him as I grabbed the sheets and covers on my side and pulled them up. I could feel his gaze on me but chose to ignore it. Right now, I'd throw a little more gasoline on that fire.

I slipped my feet into my house shoes and turned my back to him in search of my robe. Spotting it across the room, I made sure to wiggle my hips a little more than necessary as I walked toward it.

"You're pushing it," he growled, and with my back still to him, I could smile with satisfaction.

"I'm not doing anything." I looked back over my shoulder just in time to watch as his eyes raked my body. I twisted my hips and jutted my ass toward him, making it his prime focus as I bent forward and grabbed for the robe.

My eyes widened as he growled again, and before I could register what the hell was happening, my body was heaved into the air and tossed onto the bed. I bounced on impact, and then he was hovering above me, holding my wrists in his strong hands as he looked down at me with a heated stare.

"I told you that you wouldn't win." He leaned in closer

and skimmed the side of my nose with his own. "Here you are now, right back where you started."

When he kissed along my jaw and down the side of my neck, nipping and tasting along the way, I arched upward against him, and he smiled against my neck. "I don't know, Gage," I whispered, "it still feels like I'm winning."

"We both are." He shifted his hips as his lower half moved against my own, and the friction made me gasp.

He was right, we were both winning this battle.

CHAPTER 42

G *age*

WE WALKED ACROSS THE GRASS TOWARD THE IRON gate. Abby was between us, and I held one of her hands and Sawyer held the other. She was mumbling as she always does about dollies and dirt. She was the perfect mixture of sweet and tough.

Sawyer and I stared ahead, focused on our destination.

I'd come here what seemed like a million times and so had she, but this would be the first time we'd come together since the day we buried Patrick. I still felt as if the way things had worked out was so unfair, but the feeling was getting better. Today, we'd decided it was time to visit Pat as a family.

That felt strange to say, but they were my family. Frankly they had been even before everything changed, but now the word had so much meaning. I would do anything for either of them. They were mine now, to hold safe and love with everything I had.

As we stepped up to the space where we'd stood together over a year ago, I looked at Sawyer to find her looking back at me.

"It's still so hard to believe, you know," she said.

"Yeah." I looked back at the headstone, and my throat tightened I read the words etched there. *Loving husband, father, son, and friend. Remembered by his family always.*

Abigail sat on the ground and dug in the grass as I sat beside her. "Come 'ere, sis." I patted my legs and motioned for her to join me. She crawled into my lap and held up the grass she had torn away in the process.

"Pretty," she squealed, pushing it in closer to my face, and I realized she'd captured a small flower in the center of the mess in her tiny fist.

"Flower," I told her and she smiled. I lifted it to my nose. "Mm." I pretended to smell something good, yet all I could really smell was grass.

Sawyer's arm brushed against mine as she sat next to us, and together we stared ahead. The only sound was the light breeze rustling the leaves.

"We miss you, brother," I said, unsure of just how loudly I spoke. Sawyer's hand gently squeezed my forearm as she rested her head on my shoulder.

We sat there for as long as Abby would allow. When she grew tired of remaining in one place, we shifted to another, yet remained close to Pat. At one point I looked over to find Sawyer with her palm pressed against the ground as she bowed her head. Her lips moved, though I couldn't hear what she was saying.

I imagined she was sharing stories about Abigail or about their life now and how she missed him. I wasn't jealous of her love for Patrick, and I never would be. I knew she loved me, and I'd never question that, either. Patrick was and would always be a part of our lives. A man like him stayed with you, tucked safe inside the deepest part of your heart. I'd always cherish my time with him, the years I'd gotten to know him. I would also be forever grateful for the trust he had in me, and for seeing something in me that I hadn't even seen myself.

I stood near the gate with a sleepy little girl in my arms, her head resting on my shoulder as her beautiful mother walked toward us. Sawyer's blond hair blew around her shoulders and face as the breeze picked up. She focused on the ground, and with each step, I found she stood a little taller and her shoulders lifted a little more. By the time she reached us, she smiled and stepped right in to my awaiting arms.

"Is it crazy to think that he's happy for us?"

"Not at all, babe." I kissed her head, allowing my lips to remain there for a few lingering moments. "You ready to get this little one back home so she can take her nap?"

She nodded against me, and I turned around and led them back to my truck.

I'd give anything to have Patrick back so he could have the life he'd always dreamed of, even if it meant letting go of my love for Sawyer. But in his absence I swore as I walked away from him that I would honor his memory and guarantee that neither of our girls would ever feel as if they weren't my top priority.

EPILOGUE

F*ive years later*

Sawyer

I STOOD JUST OUTSIDE ABIGAIL'S ROOM, LEANING against the wall as I listened to Gage tucking in my little girl. Each time I eavesdropped on them, I fell in love with him all over again. He was such a beautiful man with an amazing heart.

He'd given us so much over the last five years that at times I felt like I would burst. Each day of our lives was inter-twined with Patrick in some way, and Gage never made me feel as if Patrick was unwelcome.

"Were you and my daddy always friends?" I closed my eyes as Abigail's sweet little voice echoed into the hall. She'd always referred to Patrick as her daddy—Gage made sure she understood that—but she called Gage her daddy too. She had two daddies, she'd tell everyone. One was in heaven and he was the angel who watched over her every day. That always brought a tear to my eye, because I, too, thought of Patrick as an angel watching over all of us. Gage, though, was Daddy Gage, her best friend, and I loved to watch them together. They had such an amazing bond and shared everything so freely.

"Your daddy was my best friend. We did everything together growing up." Gage had told her this so many times, yet I never got tired of hearing him share the funny, crazy stories of their childhood. "He was more like a brother really, because we were always side by side. We played the same sports and had the same friends. If one of us got into trouble, we both did. It didn't matter if we were actually involved, we just stood by each other through it all."

"I wish I would have been able to meet him."

I closed my eyes tighter at the sadness in Abigail's voice.

"You did, sweetheart. You were just so tiny that it's hard for you to remember." Gage was silent for a moment. "He loved you even before he met you, but that day he saw you for the first time, he was overflowing, Abby. You stole his heart. I never saw anyone with so much devotion in their eyes."

"Do you miss him?"

"I miss him every day," Gage confessed without hesitation, and my heart ached so much with the love I held for him. He was selfless and strong for the both of us. Every day he gave and gave without resistance.

I ran my hand over my stomach, feeling my son kick against my palm and smiled. Any day now, we'd meet this little angel and he, too, would be told of Patrick and how amazing he was. Though the stories would be different, of course, as he learned of Uncle Patrick and the influence he'd had on Gage.

A shadow cast over me and I looked up as Gage stepped out of Abigail's room and pulled her door closed. He looked down at where my hand remained and his grin widened. "Little man keeping you up?"

"No," I assured him, "I was just listening to the two of you talk. I love hearing the stories you share with her."

"I love telling them."

"Do you realize just how amazing you are?" I watched as the same look washed over his face that always did when I tried to tell him how great he was. "You never let me compliment you."

"Because the things I do aren't done for praise."

"And I know this," I assured him as I stepped closer and placed one hand on his forearm. "But I need you to know that I adore you and everything you give us. I love you so much, and find that each day I love you even more for every selfless act you do. Your heart is so giving, and I feel so lucky to have it."

"I'm the lucky one." Gage took my face in his hands as he pressed his lips to mine. "A beautiful wife and daughter, a son on the way. What more could any man wish for?"

"I love you, Gage Aaron Mitchell, so very much."

"And I love you too."

A year and half ago I said yes when Gage asked me to marry him. We'd spent the first four years of our relationship just living, just like Patrick wanted us to. We took Abby on trips to see the world, and we loved hard and unconditionally. We weren't afraid. We let go of the guilt and instead welcomed the memories of Pat. We brought him into our love, and even if only in spirit, he was still there.

I had a sweet little girl who reminded me every day of the love I shared with such a beautiful man. She was her daddy's girl with his dark hair and those same gorgeous eyes. Oh, and that smile. God, her smile was Patrick through and through.

I was lucky enough to have two great loves in my lifetime. One who gave me the most precious girl and taught me to love without hesitation; to go to bed each night without grudges and to live to the fullest and smile so much it made my cheeks ache.

The other love held me safely and assured me I'd always be treasured.

I'd spend the rest of life thanking my angel above for the love he shared and the life he gave me.

I'll always love you, Patrick. And now I love him too.

THANK YOU

I am still so very humbled that you, as a reader have read my story. Each day it baffles me, as I'm just a girl with a dream. I love to write, and share the worlds I've created in my mind with all that are willing to take that journey with me.

Thank you, all of you, from the bottom of my heart. Search for that epic kind of love, we all deserve to live it.

ACKNOWLEDGMENTS

KRISTIN LAZARUS-WOOD, Travis Keen, Jean Maureen Woodfin and all of your team, thank you so very much for capturing that perfect image. It is absolutely perfect. So much emotion, that epic kind of depth I was hoping for when writing this story. I needed that, hold on tight and please don't ever let go feel, and you gave it to me. I knew going in that this book needed a specific kind of cover, one that held every bit of the emotions I felt while writing it. One look at this image and I just knew. It gave me everything and more and I truly cannot thank you all enough. Perfection, and even that is not a strong enough of a word for the beauty it holds and for the talent you all have.

MELISSA GILL, MGBOOK Covers and Designs, once again you've managed to take the perfect image and make it even better. Thank you for making this cover exactly what I had hoped for and more.

THE CHARMED GIRLS, YOU ARE all amazing. The continued support you show me is something I will never be able to express just how much it means to me. Thank you all for sharing my work and for just being you. You are all the greatest bunch of ladies.

THANK YOU, LYDIA, because you are a true friend and motivator, always making me laugh and smile. We are an amazing team, and your friendship means more than I could ever express. Thank you for being one of my biggest cheerleaders and for all your hard work and dedication.

MEGAN, MY PA, you rock. You make everything so much simpler and easy for me to focus on my words. You offer me a kick when I need it and an ear when I'm stumped. You are a godsend, and I truly appreciate all you do.

BETA TEAM, YOU know who you are. Thank you all so very much for taking this journey with me. Your feedback and encouraging words along the way made this story mean so much more to me. I know this one was a hard read, and lots of tissues were involved, but you are troopers and stayed with me even though I know I'll see therapy bills int he future ;) Without you all, it wouldn't be what it is now.

TO MY HUSBAND AND children, thank you for being the best part of my days. For tolerating me when I get lost in the world of fiction and understanding that sometimes dinner may be a little late. Jayden and Tayler, no matter how many books I write, you two will always be my best creations.

MY READERS, I AM always so humbled by your support. Those random messages I received after you read my books, whether it be something big or small, I truly love them. Hearing what you think, in my eyes, is one of the greatest things about releasing a new book. I am never too busy for you.

ABOUT THE AUTHOR

C.A. Harms is a lover of HEA stories, mixed with a little heat and drama make it perfect. She needs some excitement, some angst, and moments that make her fan her face are always good too. She's an Illinois girl, born and raised. Simple and true, it honestly doesn't take much to make her happy. She loves the little things; they truly mean the most. She may have a slight addiction to her Keurig—oh my, that thing is a godsend. And so fast too. She is the mother of two children who truly are her very best friends, and their faces never fail to put a smile on her face. She has been married to her husband for eighteen years, and looks forward to many more. Even after all these years he is still able to make her heart skip a beat.

She is one of those authors that adores her fans and loves to hear from them. After all, it is because of each one of you that she continues to write.

Beside to follow her and stay up-to-date on all her upcoming release and news.

Website - https://www.authorcaharms.com/

Newsletter - http://bit.ly/1xsgHCS

 twitter.com/Charms0814

ALSO BY C. A. HARMS

Healing Hope

Ryan's Love

Whisper Forever

Made in the USA
Columbia, SC
01 November 2018